Swings and Roundabouts

Debby Fowler

A Felicity Paradise crime novel

ISBN 978 185022 241 5

Published by Truran
www.truranbooks.co.uk

Truran is an imprint of Tor Mark, United Downs
Industrial Est., St Day, Redruth TR16 5 HY

www.felicityparadise.com

The paper used for this publication has been
produced from trees that have been legally sourced from
well-managed and credibly certified forests.

Printed and bound in Cornwall by R. Booth Ltd,
The Praze, Penryn, TR10 8AA

For Di Bonce
Thank you for everything
you have done for my family

PROLOGUE

14 October, 1970, Fulham, London,

An ordinary house in an ordinary street, an ordinary day for DI Lewisham and his sergeant. It was nearly knocking-off time when over the radio came an all-too-familiar tale of suspected domestic violence reported by a neighbour – shouts, bangs, screams, slammed doors. It was not the sort of incident that Lewisham would normally have been expected to cover but he was in no hurry to go home having had a marital altercation of his own that morning which he knew meant a brooding silence all evening.

'We'll take it,' he said. 'Step on it, lad,' he said to his sergeant.

An ordinary house in an ordinary street … until Lewisham instructed his sergeant to push open the

1

front door, which was already ajar. The silence hit them first, then the smell of fresh blood, metallic, sickening ... and then the carnage, a young woman slumped in what appeared to be a crouching position as in her last moments of life. She had attempted to stretch out towards the child. The little girl, tiny, maybe six years old, lying on her back, her huge blue eyes wide open, surprised it appeared at her own appalling death ... there was blood everywhere, on the floor, on the walls, on the sofa, on the child, on the woman, a great deal on the woman.

'Jesus Christ!' managed Lewisham. He looked across at his sergeant who had turned very white. 'If you're going to be sick, lad, go outside, I don't want you contaminating the crime scene.'

The young man in question attempted a strangled noise at the back of his throat and pointed across the room. There was a photograph of an attractive family scene at a beach somewhere – Mum, Dad and twin girls. 'There are two of them,' he pointed out.

'Search the house then, lad, don't just stand there.' Going back into the hall and taking a handkerchief from his breast pocket, DI Lewisham carefully lifted the telephone and called for back-up. Moments later his sergeant clattered down the stairs.

'There's no one else up there, sir,' he reported, 'where can the other little girl be, what can have happened to her?'

'God knows,' Lewisham shrugged, then seeing the young man's expression relented a little. 'Check the garden, the garage and find the neighbour who reported the disturbance but for Christ's sake don't let her come in here.'

'Yes sir, no sir,' he swayed slightly.

'Is this your first time?' Lewisham asked.

'No, no I've …' the young man hesitated, 'it's the child, sir, I can't …'

Lewisham put a not-unfriendly hand on his shoulder. 'Buck up Penrose, how old are you?'

'Twenty-four, sir.'

'If you are going to make the police force your life's work, you are going to see quite a few dead children before you're through.'

1

15 March, 2010, Heathrow Airport

To the casual observer, the man standing by the baggage carousel could have been any age between fifty and sixty-five, stocky but clearly very fit with no hint of a beer belly or extra weight, his once dark hair strongly peppered with grey now, his eyes bright blue – a good-looking man, charismatic but with a dependable solid air about him that smacked of quiet confidence. Closer examination, however, told a different story. There were laughter lines around his eyes but he was not laughing now, there was a bowed, almost defeated air about him. He was deep in thought, so preoccupied that his case went around the carousel twice before he was apparently able to recognise it. He pushed his trolley wearily through 'Nothing to Declare' and headed for the Heathrow Express which would take him to Paddington Station and so to Cornwall. Chief

Inspector Keith Penrose was coming home.

Home – home was surely where your family lived but he had left his in Sydney – his wife, his daughter, his son, his new son-in-law and the prospect of grandchildren – how could home be anywhere but with them? He thought of each of them in turn as he settled himself into his seat and the train began to pull out of Paddington. Barbara, his wife, devoid of humour but hardworking, honest, straightforward, dependable and loyal – unlike him. He realised he had never truly loved Barbara, now he knew what true love felt like, but he had stood up in church and promised to love and honour her all his days and he had spectacularly failed to keep his promise.

He thought of his daughter Carly, who had a very special place in his heart, who had survived serious illness and ended up marrying a man of whom he could in no way disapprove. Will, his son, a chequered career in the army, a second career boat-building, and now seeing enormous opportunities in Australia, was happy and fulfilled at last. He cared for them all deeply and yet he had turned his back on them for the place he loved, the job he loved, and the woman he loved. His mind was in turmoil, his thoughts so preoccupied that it surprised him when he realised the train was already crossing Brunel's bridge over the Tamar. Cornwall – Keith let out a great sigh of relief. Despite everything, it was good to be back.

His mood quickly evaporated, however, when he reached Truro. It had been thirty-three hours since he had left Sydney, yet it seemed a lifetime ago. The family home, perched as it was on a hill above Truro, with stunning views across to the cathedral, was always a pleasing place. However, when he put his key into the door and walked into the silence, it no longer felt like his refuge, his place of safety, it felt almost alien. The family's long-term help, Becky, had been busy – the place was polished, hoovered and aired. He walked into the kitchen. On the table, there was a bowl of daffodils with a note underneath.

'Welcome home Keith, I've stocked the fridge with basics and there is one of my pies for your tea tonight. Love Becky.'

He glanced at his watch. It was seven o'clock, seven p.m. he reminded himself. He wasn't hungry but he was beyond tired, wired, restless. Automatically he walked over to the kettle, filled it, then he gazed around the room helplessly. What had he done, why was he here? As with every crisis in his life he knew there was only one solution – work. Fishing around in his jacket pocket he found his mobile; he scrolled down until he found his sergeant's number and punched it in.

'Jack,' he said, as soon as the phone was answered.

'Welcome home, sir,' came the familiar reassuring voice in response, 'I wasn't expecting to hear from you quite so soon.'

'I needed to touch base. How are things?'

'No huge dramas since you've been away, sir, I expect the villains are saving it all up until your return. There's been a few changes though …' he hesitated.

'What sort of changes?' Keith asked.

'Oh this and that,' said Jack, evasively. 'When were you planning to come back to work? They're not expecting you for a couple of days.'

'Tomorrow I thought, maybe just a half day. I expect the jetlag will catch up on me.'

'Are you tired now?' Jack asked.

'Not especially.'

'Shall we meet for a quick drink, sir? Maggie and I have had our supper.' Keith remained silent. 'Or, if you're tired I could just pop around for half an hour just to fill you in, that is if Mrs Penrose wouldn't mind?'

'Mrs Penrose isn't with me,' Keith replied, 'she is still out there.'

'Oh right,' said Jack, clearly embarrassed.

'Well, why don't I come around then, sir? I'll pick up a few beers on the way; I don't suppose you've had time to go shopping.'

'That would be good,' said Keith, and he meant it.

While he waited for Jack Curnow, Keith wandered out into his garden, shivering slightly after the warmth of Australia; the evening was surprisingly chilly. The garden was a mess. Normally it was a challenge that Keith would have relished but the sight exhausted him. He was aware of his mobile sitting heavily in his jacket pocket – there was another call he needed to make – Felicity Paradise, the love of his life – she would know he was back in Cornwall now and she would be expecting his call, but he couldn't speak to her, not yet. Somehow speaking to her felt like the ultimate betrayal of his family, even though he longed to hear her voice. He needed to sort out his plans, make decisions, reconcile the fact that he was half a world away from his family, with no immediate intention of returning to Australia. It was a mess.

The object of his thoughts was striding across Porthmeor beach as if the hounds of hell were after her, her little Jack Russell, Harvey, running ahead making his usual futile attempts to catch seagulls.

Felicity had checked the flight online, she knew the plane had arrived on time and it was hours now since Keith had been back in the UK. She longed to call him to hear his voice. It had been six weeks since they had parted at Truro station and since then her life seemed to have been on hold. They had agreed that there would be no communication between them while he was in Australia; that he would concentrate one hundred per cent on his family and his daughter's wedding; that major decisions had to be made but it was only right that she should bow out of his life while he made them.

But what had he decided? Had he returned to the UK with Barbara, had he returned alone, had he returned at all? Felicity had no way of knowing but instinctively knew it was wrong to be the first to make a move. He would tell her what was going on when he was good and ready. She trusted him implicitly to tell her how he was feeling, to tell her truthfully as to whether they had any future together, but she felt uneasy without quite knowing why: something she felt wasn't right. She glanced at her watch – five fifty-five – a long lonely evening stretched ahead. The idea of sitting, waiting for the phone to ring like some love-sick teenager, was far from appealing.

'Come on Harvey,' she called, 'let's go and see Annie.'

Cormorant Cottage had always been a haven for Felicity ever since she had first arrived in St Ives and Annie had been her landlady. The fierce, little bird-like woman had been a true friend and, well into her eighties now, she was as sharp as ever, always caring and concerned for Felicity and her family. It surprised her then when Annie answered the door and instead of the usual shriek of welcome and enormous hug said, in a none-too-welcoming manner. 'Oh, it's you, you'd better come in. Hello Harvey.'

Harvey led the way down the steps into Annie's basement kitchen which was warm and welcoming as always, even if its occupier was not. Annie went to the Aga and put the kettle on the hotplate. 'Tea, coffee?' she asked.

'Tea would be great,' said Felicity, removing her coat and sitting down on her normal chair at the kitchen table. 'How have you been, Annie?'

'Alright,' said Annie, 'and you?' Her voice was hostile; Felicity felt as if she had been slapped in the face.

'What is it, Annie, what have I done to offend you?' she asked immediately. One did not beat about the bush with Annie.

Annie appeared to ignore her, busying herself warming the old china pot, filling it with leaf tea and boiling water and then placing the tea cosy on top. She fetched two mugs from the cupboard, filled a jug with milk and placed the teapot on the table between them, all in complete silence. Then she sat down and looked across at Felicity.

'You haven't been to see me for weeks, my girl.'

'That's true,' Felicity agreed, 'I was rather preoccupied immediately after Christmas and then, I don't know, I've been doing a lot of babysitting for Mel and I'm working on a new book of illustrations ...'

'Preoccupied with your inspector?' Annie said, as she poured out the tea.

One thing Felicity had learnt over the years was the absolute pointlessness of trying to hoodwink Annie. 'Yes,' she said, 'you know about that?'

'Know about it,' said Annie, 'the whole town knows about it.'

Felicity stared at her, her eyes wide with shock. 'What do you mean, the whole town knows about it?'

'Your affair with Inspector Penrose, it's been the talk of the town.'

'But how,' said Felicity, 'how could anyone know?'

'Walking hand in hand on the beach, gazing at each other in restaurants, his car pretty much a permanent feature up at Barnoon car park,' Annie allowed herself a small grim smile. 'The Cornish aren't as thick as we're made out to be, you know. Even we can spot something that is going on if it is right under our noses.'

'And you don't approve?' Felicity said.

'Of course I don't approve, my girl.'

'But you've always teased me about him, almost encouraging me.'

'That was just a bit of fun,' said Annie, 'I wasn't serious and I didn't expect you to be.'

'But you're always telling me I need a man in my life.'

'Yes,' Annie agreed, 'but not someone else's man.'

'Oh, I see,' said Felicity, 'so this is about Keith being married?'

'Of course it's about Keith being married. I'm a chapel-goer as you know, my girl, and it doesn't sit easy with me, you walking off with somebody else's husband.'

'But it isn't like that,' said Felicity.

'So tell me what it is like,' Annie demanded.

'Keith's wife, Barbara, left him. She went off to Australia last autumn to visit their daughter.'

'Well, that's fair enough,' said Annie, 'the man is always working, I expect she felt like a change of scene. People do go and visit their grown-up children, it doesn't mean their marriage is over.'

'Keith thinks that she won't come back, at least that was his view when he went out there in February for their daughter Carly's wedding.'

'She's married an Australian then?'

Felicity shook her head. 'No, she and her boyfriend went out to Australia a couple of years ago. He is a marine biologist and she is a physiotherapist, they had no problem finding work and absolutely love it, they're definitely going to make their lives there and it looks like Keith's wife might too.'

'And Keith?'

'He doesn't want to leave Cornwall or his job.'

Annie was silent for a moment. 'His job can't be going on for much longer, how old is he?'

'Sixty-four,' Felicity said.

'Old enough to have more sense,' Annie murmured. 'So he is a Cornishman, through and through, I'll give him that, but with his job nearing its end, the only thing that can really be keeping him in this country is you. Do you think it's right to keep a man from his family? There will be grandchildren soon. Do you think it's right that he will hardly ever get to know them? Think what pleasure Minty and Charlie bring you, imagine life without them, imagine they were living the other side of the world.'

'Stop it Annie,' Felicity said, desperately close to tears.

Annie stretched out her hand, small, frail and bony, and took one of Felicity's in hers. She studied Felicity in silence for a moment. 'See here, my bird, you're a very attractive woman. You look years younger than your age, you've kept your figure and you have a lovely complexion, so few lines. You must have been a beautiful young woman and you're still a very attractive one now. OK, your dress sense is a bit strange,' Annie relented a little and smiled properly for the first time.

Felicity looked down a little self-consciously at her trademark multi-coloured sweater, purple trousers and bright red Converse shoes.

'You don't act your age,' Annie continued, 'you're good fun and I know you're lonely. You deserve a good man to love you after all these years of widowhood but not that man, he is not yours to have.'

'He seems to think he is,' Felicity said, miserably.

'Well he's wrong, my girl, and the sooner you realise it, the better.'

Keith and Jack sat in the gathering gloom in what Barbara called the conservatory but in reality was really little more than a lean-to greenhouse which they had added to the back of the house some years before. They were sitting in two wicker chairs, feet on the table, just embarking on their third beer.

They had spent the last half hour discussing the various cases which had been outstanding when Keith had left five weeks before.

'So nothing much has kicked off in my absence,' said Keith.

Jack smiled. 'Cheers, sir,' he said, raising his bottle, 'no, as I said to you on the phone, the villains are waiting for you to return.'

Keith took a sip of his beer. Unlike his sergeant he had to drink it out of a glass, he couldn't bear drinking beer straight from a bottle, which in turn reminded him of Australia. The image came to him of the last family barbecue they had shared together, what two, three days ago? Despite the sun, the sea, the surf, the delicious smells wafting over the beach from Carly's barbecue, despite the beer especially poured into a glass for his benefit, despite the laughter, the sense of family all around him, it had felt more like a wake than a party. He forced his mind back to concentrate on the present.

'You mentioned on the phone, Jack, that there were some changes going on.'

'Yes …' Jack hesitated, 'there's been some redundancies.'

'Really, many?'

'About eight at the station.'

'Good God, that's quite a cull. Is your job alright?'

Jack nodded. 'Yes fine, thank goodness.'

'So who are they letting go?'

Jack reeled off a list of names.

'That's odd,' said Keith, 'there's quite a few there who are nowhere near retirement.'

'It's the thirty-year rule,' Jack said, hesitantly. 'Anyone who has been in the force for more than thirty years can be asked to retire early.'

'I see,' said Keith. The silence stretched between them, both knowing that Keith had been a policeman for more than forty years, never mind thirty. Keith felt a cold hand clutch at his heart, there was a sudden tingling down the back of his spine. Losing his family was bad enough, losing his job was unthinkable, a nightmare. He was a policeman, that was what he was, who he was, it defined him. Stripped of that identity he had no idea if there would be anything left.

2

By lunchtime the following day Keith was ready for bed. He had rung the family to tell them he had arrived home safely and there was really nothing at the station which required his immediate attention. In fact, it had been a tedious morning. Jack had used the period while he was away to dramatically tidy his office with the result that he could find nothing. He found the order and cleanliness of the place alarming and he had done his best to mess it up.

'I have a little brother just like you,' Jack observed when he came in with a coffee mid-morning.

'How come?' Keith asked.

'My poor mum would tidy up his room, day after day, week after week, while he was at school and then Steve came home and within five minutes the place would be destroyed again,' Jack smiled. 'He's at uni now, my mother refuses to go near his accommodation, she can't bear to think what it must be like.'

'Oh great,' said Keith, 'so you're suggesting I'm like some messy teenager with no sense of responsibility?'

'The cap does sort of fit, sir,' said Jack, hurriedly backing out of the door.

By two o'clock Keith was just about to tell Jack that he was off for the day when a call came through on his direct line.

'Is that Chief Inspector Keith Penrose?'

'Yes,' said Keith.

'My name is Graham Sinclair.' Keith noted the slight Scottish accent. 'I'm with the Intelligence Office, at the Met.'

'Oh yes,' said Keith.

'We're reinvestigating a cold case and we were wondering if you might be able to give us a hand. It's important; we think we may have a serial killer on the loose.'

'I'd be pleased to help,' said Keith, his interest quickening, 'how long ago are we talking about?'

'Well that's just it sir, forty years ago, in fact you're the only officer on the original case who is still alive.'

'Oh great,' said Keith, 'that really does a lot for my self-esteem.'

'You must have been very young at the time, sir,' Graham Sinclair said tactfully, 'you may not even remember it – it's the Johnson case?' At the mention of the name, images flashed into Keith's mind. Involuntarily he took a sharp intake of breath, trying to steady himself. 'Are you still there?' Graham asked after a moment.

'Yes,' said Keith, 'and yes, of course, I do remember the Johnson case, I will always remember the Johnson case.'

'There have been no similar cases in the intervening years, either in London, or anywhere else in the country … that is until last Thursday.'

'Hang on a moment,' said Keith, 'this doesn't make any sense. Surely whoever was responsible for the Johnson murders would be too old to commit murder again; he's probably dead by now. You said yourself the investigating officers were all deceased except me and I was just a young lad. Surely you're not suggesting that the man who killed Mrs Johnson and her daughter is still at large, and after forty years has started killing again?'

'You're still a serving police officer, sir. May I ask how old you were at the time of the Johnson murder?'

'I was about twenty-four,' said Keith.

'Supposing the murderer had been say, twenty when he killed the Johnsons, he could still be capable of murder now, he might only be sixty.'

'I suppose so,' said Keith, 'it just seems highly improbable.'

'There is a particular element to this new case,' Graham Sinclair said.

'Go on,' said Keith.

'There's another missing child. That's what makes us connect it to the Johnsons.'

Keith already felt sick to the stomach. He didn't really want to know any more but he forced himself to ask. 'So what are the details?'

'Mother and son, the boy was two, both killed in their home just off Gloucester Road in Fulham – a nice family. The husband was away on business but the boy had a sister who is seven, and she has gone missing. Her name is Fiona, Fiona McAllister.'

'Like Janey Johnson?'

'Like Janey Johnson, sir,' Graham agreed.

After he had finished the call Keith returned to his desk and sat down heavily in his chair, swivelling around to gaze at the car park below with unseeing eyes. The Johnson case had haunted him all his working life, not simply because of the murder, but more because Janey Johnson, the missing child, had never been found. If the killer could do what he had done to her mother and sister, Keith could not bear to imagine what Janey's fate had been, and now it appeared the nightmare had started again after all these years … and yet it was so hard to imagine a serial killer repeating his crime after such a long period. All that mattered on an immediate basis was to find this new missing little girl, Fiona McAllister. The Met had managed to keep the story out of the press for the last thirty-six hours, fearing that over-exposure might panic the killer into murdering Fiona. Keith suspected that the poor child was already dead, but while there was any sort of hope …

He had agreed to travel up to New Scotland Yard the following day and go through the files with Graham Sinclair to see if there was anything that might help the new case. This re-emergence of the Johnson nightmare seemed, suddenly, too much to bear. The pain of leaving his family in Australia, his apparent inability to contact Felicity Paradise, his concerns over his career and now this. His mind flitted back to what he could remember of the case, which was pretty much everything. He glanced at his watch, it was three o'clock now, time to go home. He stood up, stooped with weariness like an old man. He would go to bed as soon as he got home but he had a feeling that exhausted though he was, sleep would elude him.

The following morning while Keith was once again on a train but this time heading to Paddington, his sergeant, Jack Curnow, was summoned by the Chief Superintendent, George Staple. Jack had never been inside the 'Super's' office before – that was his boss's job, keeping the 'Super' happy. He was beyond nervous when he was shown in, his mind looping through the events of the last few weeks trying to think what it was he could possibly have done wrong. George Staple stood up and offered him a hand, a big dour burly policeman with a formidable reputation.

'Don't look so worried, Curnow,' George said, 'you're not in any trouble. Sit down.'

With relief Jack sank into a chair. 'Thank you, sir,' he mumbled.

'In fact I've had nothing but good reports of you,' George continued. 'I think some promotion is in order. If you work hard and continue the way you're going, there is no reason why you shouldn't make Inspector within the next five years.'

'I'd like that sir, certainly I'll work very hard to achieve it …' He hesitated.

'I sense a "but" coming,' said George Staple.

'I know Chief Inspector Penrose isn't long off retirement now, sir, and I'd like to see him through to the end, until he retires that is. I reckon we're quite a good team.'

'Your loyalty is commendable,' said George Staple, thoughtfully, 'and I think we can probably plan around it.'

Jack was surprised, he had expected an argument. 'Thank you, sir. Is there anything else?'

'No,' said George, and stood up to shake the young man's hand again. Jack headed towards the door. 'Oh, just one thing Curnow, how is Chief Inspector Penrose?'

'He's fine sir,' Jack said, 'a bit jet-lagged and then he has had to go back up to London today to help the Met with a cold case.'

'Yes, I heard about that,' said George, 'awful business. Did he bring his wife back with him from Australia?'

Jack shook his head. 'No, Mrs Penrose has stayed out there.'

'Has she plans to return?'

'I'm not sure,' said Jack, 'it's a bit of a tricky subject, we haven't really discussed it.'

'No, no, I quite understand, but he could do with her being around just now.'

A few minutes later, Jack sat thoughtfully in front of his computer screen, replaying in his mind the 'Super's' words. He didn't like it – there had been no suggestion of a fight about him staying on until Keith retired, and why would Keith need his wife around him now? There could be only one explanation – Keith was going to be given early retirement, and from his colleagues who had shared the same fate, Jack knew this meant that Keith only had three months left as a working policeman.

While Jack was contemplating his boss's future with some trepidation, Felicity Paradise was marching along the cliff path heading toward Clodgy Point. The path was slippery with mud from recent rain and heavy going, but trying not to lose her footing was at least keeping her mind occupied. It was a mad March Hare day, bright sunshine, clouds scudding across the sky, the wind strong and gusty, yet it was warm and spring was all around her, the sea a piercing blue. She should have been feeling optimistic after the last long dark weeks, but of course, she was still waiting. If Keith hadn't changed his flight he would have been home now two days ago, and if so, why hadn't he been in touch? There seemed to Felicity only two possible explanations – either he had come back with his wife, Barbara or he had not come back at all. A reconciliation with his wife should make her pleased for him, she thought. If I truly love this man then I have to recognise that among his many qualities is one of loyalty. If he has found a way to stay within the bosom of his family that has to be the right thing for him.

Felicity found a boulder and sat down on it, facing the sun and the sea; it was truly gorgeous. Harvey looked at her reproachfully; he considered walks were for walking, not lounging around in the sun.

She called him over and scratched him behind his ear, but he wasn't interested, there were too many good smells and always the possibility of a rabbit to chase. Felicity thought about her own family, her son James, usually called Jamie, and his two boys, her daughter Mel and her two children. Was there anyone who could persuade her to leave her children and grandchildren and live the other side of the world? That was what she had expected Keith to do, how selfish she had been. Annie was right, it was asking too much. Love had blinded her as to what was right and wrong, he was not hers, he never would be. The four weeks they had spent together had been the happiest of her life and she had them to hold on to as a treasured memory. She had to be strong; she would have to learn to cope without him in her life. She rose to her feet shakily, and putting a hand to her face realised she was crying. She called Harvey and began stumbling back down the cliff path towards St Ives.

Graham Sinclair's office was a miserable affair, a box of a room, with one tiny, grimy window which sported panoramic views of the wall of another building about three feet away. Graham Sinclair proved to be a short, wiry man in his mid-forties, his mass of red hair in tune with his accent. He shook Keith warmly by the hand. 'Coffee?' he asked.

Keith hesitated. A veteran of Met coffee, he wasn't sure he could cope.

'I have my own percolator,' Graham confided.

'I'll have one then,' said Keith, 'thank you.'

While Graham busied himself making two mugs of coffee, Keith gazed listlessly out of the tiny window. He felt absolutely exhausted, he had hardly slept the night before, he dared not even begin to imagine what time it was in Australia.

'Sugar?' Graham asked.

'No thanks,' said Keith, pulling himself together. 'I've just flown in from Australia a couple of days back, so forgive me if I'm not at my best.'

'Good Lord,' said Graham, 'so you've been down to Cornwall and now I've dragged you back up to London again?'

'I'm happy to help, or try to,' said Keith, and meant it.

'I've booked you into the hotel around the corner,' said Graham, 'I thought a couple of nights would do it.'

Keith looked startled. 'Oh, I hadn't realised you'd want me to stay over, I've brought nothing with me.'

'Sorry,' said Graham, 'I should have mentioned it. I thought we'd spend today de-briefing you on what you can remember of the case and then, I thought I'd set you to work on the files to see if there was anything in the MO reports that you can link together to help us. We've been through it a thousand times ourselves, of course, but you were there that first time and seeing it with fresh eyes you might just spot something. It's certainly worth doing; to be frank, we have little else to go on. Have you seen the papers this morning?'

'Yes,' said Keith.

'Well, the powers that be upstairs are hopping mad, they need this solved. Two dead children, two missing and we're no nearer solving the crimes than we were on the day you discovered the Johnson bodies …' He hesitated. 'Could we start there, Chief Inspector Penrose?'

'Keith,' Keith suggested.

'OK Keith, that's great, let's go. So it was you and DI Chris Lewisham who found the bodies?'

Keith nodded. 'Yes.'

'Were you expecting a murder scene?'

'Absolutely not,' said Keith, 'there was a report of a domestic and it was only because it was on our route back to the station, we said we would take it.'

'It was reported by a neighbour?'

'Yes,' said Keith, 'a Mrs …'

'Maber,' Graham supplied.

'Yes, that's right. Long dead of course?'

Graham nodded. 'Did she actually see anything?'

'No, no, she heard a lot of shouting and then she thought she heard a scream and it was the scream that prompted her to call the police. She said there had been no trouble of any sort before, although Caroline Johnson, the mother, the victim and her husband, Thomas, were no longer living together.'

'But Thomas was not a suspect?'

'No, he was the obvious suspect initially, particularly since one of the little girls was missing but he was in Washington DC at the time with plenty of witness corroboration. The marriage was on the rocks because of his move to the US, I think. Is he still alive?'

'We think so but we haven't contacted him at the moment. There seems no point in putting an old man through painful memories yet again, unless we think there was anything he can add to the case. You met him, of course?'

'Yes, on many occasions,' said Keith, 'he flew over the moment he heard the news. There was no question of him being any sort of suspect, his alibi was cast-iron, he couldn't have been there.'

'And other male members of the family or boyfriends of Caroline Johnson?'

'You must have all this on the file.'

'I have,' said Graham, 'I'd just like to hear it from you to see if there is something here we've missed.'

'Although Thomas and Caroline Johnson's marriage had been finished for over two years, it appeared that Mrs Johnson had no new love interest in her life. She worked part-time on a woman's magazine but most of her energies went into raising her two little girls. She had a sister and a nephew I think.'

'Yes, that's right, but you never saw them as a suspects?'

'No,' said Keith, 'not as far as I remember.'

'Were you able to establish whether Janey was injured before she was taken?'

Keith shook his head. 'Obviously all the blood – and there was a lot of it – was analysed for blood groups, but of course it was long before DNA. Mrs Johnson hadn't been raped, there were no fingerprints to help us, obviously the killer had used gloves.'

'We still have the blood-stained clothes. I suppose it might be possible to run DNA tests, if Janey's blood was in evidence at the crime scene.'

'You won't be able to do that,' said Keith.

'Why not?' Graham asked.

'They were identical twins. I've become something of an expert on identical twins, I had a case not so long ago.'

Graham frowned. 'I don't understand.'

'Identical twins share the same DNA; the only

way you can tell them apart forensically is by their fingerprints. No two people in the world share the same fingerprints, even identical twins, but their DNA would be a perfect match.'

Graham paused while he digested this. 'So there were no witness sightings of anyone coming in or out of the house?' he asked at last.

'No,' said Keith, 'Caroline, Mrs Johnson, had picked up both girls from school. There was evidence on the kitchen table that they had eaten their tea and were settling down to do a bit of homework. By the time we reached the scene it was dusk. It had been a grey day and it was getting dark early. It was a quiet residential street which mostly contained families; the children were home from school and working parents were not yet back from work – a quiet period in the afternoon.'

'You'd have thought if the surviving twin, Janey, had seen what had happened to her mother and sister, she'd have screamed the place down if the killer had tried to take her out of the house alive?'

Keith nodded. 'I've been round and round it a thousand times. Janey was definitely in the house for tea and then apparently disappeared off the face of the earth. I've always assumed that one day her body would be found when a house was demolished, or a new road dug, new trees planted in a park but no, nothing. It was a huge failure on our part.'

'There were no arrests?'

'No,' said Keith, 'and there were no suspects, no real suspects. We hauled in everyone for questioning with the slimmest of connections to the family. While the body of Janey remained undiscovered we were in a desperate battle against time, hoping we were going to find her alive …' his voice trailed away. 'Are you going to tell me about this new family, the McAllisters?'

'In good time,' said Graham, 'I want to finish with the Johnsons first. Did you have a pet theory?'

Keith shook his head. 'I don't understand why he took Janey, there was no hint of sexual activity relating to either the mother or Katie the dead twin. They had been brutally murdered but it was like an execution, somehow cold, devoid of passion. So why let one child live? If we were dealing with a paedophile it would have made sense, but there was no evidence to suggest that. We interviewed everyone, everyone we could think of who had committed any sort of crime against a child, those in and out of prison. We interviewed any villain in the area who had ever committed a violent assault, none of us slept for weeks, we left no stone unturned. It finished Chris Lewisham really, he took early retirement. We arrived so soon after it had happened, less than twenty minutes they

31

reckoned at the lab. We should have been able to track down who was responsible.'

'Let's go for a spot of lunch, then you can check into your hotel and buy the few things you need to stay over, then I'll give you the McAllister file.'

'Just give me a desk and a sandwich,' said Keith. 'There's a missing child, I don't think we have time for lunch.'

3

By seven-thirty that evening Keith could do no more. He had spent all afternoon studying the McAllister files, cross-referencing them with the Johnson case. He had asked endless questions, and recognising that he would not be able to take the files out of the building, had made copious notes. Apart from a brief break to buy some toiletries, he had not left his desk. At five-thirty Graham Sinclair had headed home and suggested that Keith should give himself a break but he could not, he felt like a man possessed.

Later, after an indifferent dinner in the hotel's charmless restaurant, he had moved to the bar, an altogether cosier place, and installed himself in a quiet corner with a coffee and a brandy. Physically he was exhausted. His back ached and it was an effort to move, but his mind was still whirling and he understood why. Janey Johnson had haunted him for most of his adult life. The murder of the Johnson family was terrible but it had already been committed by the time he and Lewisham arrived on the scene – there was nothing that he could do to help mother and daughter other than try and track down their killer. It was the missing little girl and what terrible fate had awaited her that he could never get out of his mind. He had not saved her. This new case was giving him a second chance to put things right; no, he thought, there was nothing he could do forty years later to redress the loss of Janey, but at least if they could find little Fiona, it would heal the wound a little ... perhaps paper over some of the scars.

He looked at the pages of notes he had made during the day, his tired eyes barely focusing. Both cases were so astonishingly similar. Both murders involved stabbing the mother and a child, both families lived in the same area, and creepily the three girls, despite a forty-year gap, had attended the same school, a private school called Westways just off the King's Road. From the file and discussions with Sinclair, Keith had established that this connection had been made and a visit to the school had already taken place. There was only one employee left at the school who had been there when the Johnson tragedy had occurred. She was a cleaner who had been just a teenager at the time and clearly was outside the frame of their investigation. In both cases there had been no forced entry into the houses, suggesting that the killer had made a plausible case for his arrival on the doorstep – and then there was this inexplicable, unbelievable forty-year gap. To Keith Penrose, despite the similarities, it still seemed inconceivable that someone who had committed such a brutal murder forty years ago, could have gone on to lead a blameless life in the interim … until now. It had already been established that there was no actual link between the two families, no mutual relatives or even friends. Apart from their ghastly end, there was no common denominator, other than the school.

The search for Fiona McAllister had already gone global. Modern communications had made that part of the investigation so much easier than the search for Janey. The borders were under surveillance, all airports, ports and the Channel Tunnel on red alert. Every police force in the country was on the look-out for Fiona, across Europe and beyond. Since his arrival in London, the media had flashed out the story and the little girl's face was everywhere, but, thought Keith, one only had to think of recent high-profile cases to recognise that even international coverage was no guarantee of finding a missing child.

Unlike the Johnsons, the McAllister family

appeared to be close-knit. Parents, Moira and Ian, seemed to have had a strong marriage and doted on their two children, Fiona and Ed. Ian McAllister had been away for the night on business, staying in Manchester. At the exact time of the murders he was in the middle of a very complex boardroom row with over twenty people able to confirm his whereabouts. His complete collapse at the disintegration of his family and his desperate attempts to find his missing daughter, scouring the streets night and day, all rang true. In similar circumstances I would be out of my mind, Keith thought and Ian McAllister's reported behaviour were those of an innocent man driven mad with grief and shock. Keith drained his brandy glass and looked up at the bar, contemplating another.

His eyes were drawn to a couple sitting at a small table by the imitation log fire at the far end of the room. They were not young, fifty, Keith supposed and they were gazing into one another's eyes, holding hands oblivious of everything around them except one another. The sight of them was like a body blow to Keith and the resulting sense of pain and loss made him almost gasp aloud. Why hadn't he been in touch with Felicity, what was going on his head? She must be wondering what had happened to him, but then again, why hadn't she contacted him? No, that was ridiculous, it was obvious that he had to make the first move on his return from Australia. For all Felicity knew, he had bought Barbara back with him. He suddenly couldn't bear the sight of the happy couple another moment. He would forego the second brandy, a good idea in any event. Gathering up his notes he headed across the bar to bed.

'It's awful, isn't it, Mum, this missing little girl?' Mel was sitting at the kitchen table the paper spread out in front of her. She looked up at her mother through a curtain of blonde hair. Felicity was busy chopping onion for a shepherd's pie.

'I heard it on the news briefly as I was driving over,' said Felicity, 'but I must admit I turned off the radio half way through, I couldn't bear to listen to any more.'

'Her family has been murdered, well at least her mother and brother are dead, and her brother was only two,' Mel said, 'and the little girl, Fiona, seems to have disappeared off the face of the earth. Their ages – it could be Charlie and Minty.'

'Don't,' said Felicity, 'don't even think such dreadful thoughts.' She paused in her chopping and regarded her daughter for a moment. The clever, feisty, demanding child, teenager and young woman had softened dramatically with the birth of her children. Her father would hardly recognise her,

Felicity thought. She smiled at her daughter. 'That's the trouble with having children, it makes you so vulnerable. I suppose it's the father who did it; these awful crimes are normally a family affair.'

'No, no, not in this case,' said Mel, 'the father is in the clear, he was up in Manchester.'

'Poor, poor man then,' Felicity said.

'In fact,' said Mel, continuing to read the paper, 'they say there are similarities with a case which happened forty years ago, it could be a serial killing.'

'A serial killing with a forty-year gap, hardly likely, is it?' Felicity said. 'The original killer would be an old man by now.'

'They're making the link,' said Mel, '… in fact, good heavens!'

'What?' Felicity asked.

'Hang on a second,' Mel frowned in concentration as she read the paper, 'your inspector is involved.'

Felicity stopped chopping. She turned her back on Mel and gazed out of the window in the pretence of seeing something of interest there. The Hayle estuary was laid out before her, it was a beautiful morning with a slight mist rising off the water, the sun still apricot, sending pink streaks across the water. 'What do you mean,' she managed in what she hoped was a normal and casual voice, 'my inspector is involved?'

'It says here Chief Inspector Keith Penrose of Devon and Cornwall Police has been asked to help with the McAllister murders because of his involvement with the Johnson case forty years ago. So the previous murders must have happened in Cornwall.'

'No, no,' said Felicity, 'when Keith started out with the police he trained with the Met, so the first murders would probably have happened in London too.'

'I hadn't realised he was back,' said Mel. 'How is he?'

'We haven't had a chance to catch up since he got back,' said Felicity, keeping her voice steady.

'Well it sounds as though he'll be based in London for a bit until this little girl is found, or not …' her voice trailed off.

Felicity returned her attention to the onion. So perhaps that was why he hadn't been in touch. He had come back from Australia and straight into this hunt for a missing child. Man's inhumanity to children was always the thing that got to Keith Penrose, he couldn't bear it when a child was hurt, killed, abused – it affected him deeply, Felicity knew. Dredging up this forty-year old case where one child had been murdered and the other missing would certainly be taking its toll, but was he really so busy that he could not spare five minutes, even for a quick call just to tell her he was back?

She remembered, suddenly, a day that she and Keith had spent together shortly before he had left for Australia. Mel had been called to attend an emergency court hearing and had asked Felicity to baby-sit both children for the day. The children had adored Keith. The image flashed into her mind of Keith sitting by her Aga with Charlie on his knee, while he answered in a most serious and adult way which children love, the many questions that Minty had for him. He was so relaxed with them, so happy in their company. This new case had to be crucifying him, so why didn't he need to talk to her? There could only be one explanation – Keith must have brought his wife home with him and was trying to find a way to tell Felicity that their relationship was over.

Some hours later James Paradise put down the receiver thoughtfully, having been the last member of his family to speak to his mother when she had telephoned for a chat. He wandered through to the kitchen. The boys had finished their supper and having spoken to their grandmother, had disappeared hurriedly upstairs before someone mentioned homework. His wife, Trish, stood over the kitchen sink washing up. He came up behind her and put his arms around her, resting his chin on her shoulder.

'What's up, Jamie?' Trish asked, as ever, perfectly in tune with his feelings.

'Did you think Mum was OK?' he asked, anxiously.

Trish took her hands out of the sink, dried them on the towel and swivelled round to face her husband, smiling up at him and drawing him close. The happiness of their marriage never failed to astound them both. They had been married for seventeen years and of course there had been cross words and misunderstandings but they were so close, closer than ever, and everyone including themselves thought it was extraordinary that they could not only live together, raise children together, but also work together.

'It's that policeman,' said Trish.

'What, Penrose?'

'Chief Inspector Penrose,' Trish corrected him with a smile. 'Mel says they spent a lot of time together at the beginning of the year. Apparently his wife had gone off to Australia and then he followed her out there for some family wedding. Your mother has been as grumpy as hell ever since, Mel says she snaps at everyone, very tetchy.'

'God, she's not having an affair with him, is she?' said Jamie, clearly appalled.

'It's amazing, isn't it?' said Trish, 'it doesn't matter what age you are, children cannot bear the concept of their parents having sex.'

'It's not that,' Jamie protested.

'Yes it is, you're just like the boys. I've only got to put one arm round you and they start making vomiting noises.'

'That's true, but they're teenagers,' said Jamie firmly. 'I'd like Mum not to be alone, I'd like her to have someone in her life, but definitely not a married man – that is sure to end in heartbreak, hers not his. She deserves better. What is he like anyway, this Chief Inspector?'

'I don't know,' said Trish, 'having never met him, but Mel and Martin like him, Martin particularly, I think.'

'Well, I hope he is not going to hurt Mum, she's been through enough with Dad dying and then Gilla.'

Trish gave him a squeeze. 'She is pretty grown-up and fairly streetwise, your mum. I'm sure she can take care of herself.'

'No one is streetwise when it comes to affairs of the heart,' said Jamie. 'Look at me, blinded by love I ended up being stuck with you.'

'That's true,' said Trish, laughing, 'and thank God for it.'

4

'The train is now approaching Truro, Truro will be the next station stop.'

Keith stood up and reached for his briefcase, he had spent most of the journey staring out of the window with sightless eyes trying to stretch his tired brain into some form of lateral thinking. It was day five since Fiona had gone missing and, as far as he could tell, the Met were no closer to finding her or the killer than they had been on day one. The Johnson case happening, as it had done, so near to the beginning of his career had profoundly affected him for years, still did, and now here was a copycat crime happening close to the end of his career – the irony was not lost on him. Truro Cathedral came into view as the train slowed for the station. Normally the sight cheered him but today it did not. An optimistic man, with boundless energy, depression was not something Keith had ever really experienced and therefore did not recognise. He knew he felt tired and listless, he knew he was feeling hopelessly inadequate when it came to helping find Fiona McAllister, but he did not know why he felt these things. There was no longer any joy in coming home nor even going to work, come to that. He trudged out of the station, across the potholed car park to his car, stepping in a puddle as he went and cursing his wet foot. He had just reached the car when his mobile rang.

'Keith, it's George Staple, are you back from London yet?'

'Just arrived, sir,' said Keith.

'I wondered if you could pop into my office, say in half an hour?'

'Will do, sir,' Keith said, glancing at his watch. That was all he needed, a meeting with the 'Super' who no doubt was going to ask him what progress he had made in assisting the Met. The answer was so painfully simple – none.

Chief Superintendent George Staple could not remember a time in his career when he had felt so uncomfortable – no, it was worse than that. He sat staring at his blotter, feeling downright miserable. He had hardly slept the night before for worry, turning over and over in his mind the right words, when the reality was painfully obvious – there were no right words. Keith Penrose was announced by George's anxious-looking secretary, Brenda, who was only too aware of what was to come. As usual, Keith entered George's office with great speed and energy; the man really did belie his years. It was a mad decision to let go a man of Keith's experience, so full of intelligence and downright decency and an extraordinary skill at winkling out the villains. His seemingly bottomless well of compassion for man's frailties was all the more extraordinary given he had chosen a profession which tended to show mankind at its very worst.

George rose to his feet slowly, extending his hand, mumbled a greeting and plastering on his face what he hoped appeared something like a smile. Keith took his hand, returning the smile, and then the expression on his face froze. Christ, he knows already, George thought, fleetingly, but that of course was what he was trained to do, to read other people's thoughts and plug into their true feelings.

'Sit down, Keith,' George said, indicating the chair. George Staple had two seating areas in his office. There were a couple of easy chairs around a coffee table in the window across the far side of the room. When visiting officers were shown to this spot they knew they were in for a fairly easy ride. However when they were shown to the chair opposite his desk, it was serious, like being summoned to the head teacher's study. Keith sat across from his boss's desk now, his mind unravelling with panic.

'So how were things up at the Met,' George asked conversationally, 'are you getting anywhere?'

'That's not why you asked me here, is it, sir?' Keith said.

'No,' George replied, 'Keith, you know there's been ...' he hesitated, seeming unable to find the words. Despite the awfulness of the moment Keith could not bear to see him suffer. 'You're trying to find a way to tell me I have to take early retirement,' Keith said.

'I'm terribly sorry,' said George, clearly meaning it. 'I just, I just ...' he paused, 'Oh God, I can't even get this right. It's the thirty-year rule, you see, they're kicking out virtually everyone who has served in the police force for more than thirty years. It's a mad decision; it means a great number of top officers at the peak of their abilities are losing their jobs.'

'I suppose I should be grateful,' said Keith, 'I've managed to spend over forty years in the force.'

George Staple remained silent; he could think of nothing to say.

'How long have I got?' Keith asked after a moment.

'Three months,' said George, 'until the end of June. Keith, I'm making such a hash of this. I know what your job means to you, I've been up all night worrying about it. I fought to keep you, fought hard but there is no bending of the rules, even for a man of your calibre. It's appalling, I am sorry.'

This was a side of his boss Keith had never seen before, the man behind the mask, he had always thought of him as being rather a dry old stick but the man clearly had feelings that ran deeper than he had ever imagined.

'And I'm sorry to have been responsible for you losing your beauty sleep, sir,' Keith said, with a gentle smile. There was no sarcasm or bitterness in his words.

'You're taking it remarkably well,' said George, puzzled.

I'm not, Keith thought. I'm in free-fall, I can't bear it, but to George he said, 'There's no point in doing anything else, is there, sir? If I ask you to reconsider the decision, you would be powerless to help, your hands are tied.'

'They are, I'm afraid,' said George, 'there is really no alternative, it's a directive that has to be carried out.'

'Only obeying orders,' Keith said, not unkindly.

George nodded his head. 'Something like that.'

'Well sir,' said Keith getting to his feet, 'if I've

only got three more months to catch the bad guys, I had better get on with it.'

'Would you like to have a cup of coffee and talk some more?' George asked. Clearly the relief that Keith was taking the news so well was written all over his face.

'No, no, I'm fine thank you, sir.'

'We'll have a party,' George said, 'a good send-off for you.'

Keith stopped in his tracks on the way to the door. 'I'm not sure,' he said, 'can we put that one on hold? I'm not at all certain I would like that.'

'Alright,' said George, 'we'll leave it up to you to decide, of course, and take as much time as you need to help the Met with this case you're working on. It would be a wonderful finale for you if you could make the breakthrough and I don't mind admitting it would do Devon and Cornwall no harm either.' George Staple was already in recovery.

'Thank you, sir,' said Keith, and let himself quietly out of the door.

He couldn't face going back to the office, couldn't stand the thought of having to tell Jack. He walked straight to his car and without any apparent forethought simply drove onto the roundabout and turned left towards Malpas. He drove along the edge of the Truro River until he found a parking space. Having parked up, he got out of the car and found a park bench overlooking the water. The tide was out, the sun glinted on the mudflats, the boats lolled lazily on their keels, a heron flapped across his field of vision and disappeared around the bend of the river. He knew he had been expecting this day ever since Jack had told him of the redundancies, yet the shock he felt came in fast, hitting him in waves. He could barely remember life before he was a policeman. What had he been before … a child? In three months' time he would be a policeman no longer, it was unthinkable. He knew he needed to share this burden with someone and there were really only two choices – his wife, who would be delighted at the news having always hated his career, or … Felicity.

It was not really a choice. He felt around in his jacket pocket for his mobile; he had a signal. With a hand which he noticed was trembling, he selected her number.

'It's me,' he said, when she answered.

'I know,' she replied.

'Is that because your famous sixth sense has kicked in?'

'No,' said Felicity, 'your name comes up on my mobile screen when you call me.'

'What does it say,' Keith asked, '"Prize pillock"?'

'No, "Inspector P",' Felicity replied.

'That's rather formal, isn't it?'

'I didn't know you very well when I first saved your number.'

'And now?' Keith asked.

There was a pause; when she spoke at last there was a break in her voice. 'I don't know whether I know you any better now, or even if I am allowed to know you at all.'

'Can we meet?' Keith asked, acutely aware suddenly of the pain he must have caused her.

'When?'

'Now?'

'I'm not sure,' Felicity began.

'I really need to talk to you.'

'Me too, I suppose,' she admitted.

'I'm sorry I haven't been in touch, I've been so confused …' he hesitated, 'and busy.'

'I saw from the paper that you are involved in that dreadful murder up in London. I know how much you hate crimes against children, it must be awful. Do you want to come here? I'm at home at the moment.'

'Oh please,' said Keith, 'yes please.'

Some of Felicity's spirit returned. 'Well, Chief Inspector, Harvey and I had better go and roll out the red carpet.'

5

He still had the key to her front door on his key ring, but when he reached the mad purple door to Felicity's home, Jericho Cottage, it was already ajar. He entered quietly, closing the door gently behind him, but at the sound of the lock clicking shut, Harvey came bounding down the stairs, yelping with delight. Keith bent down to fuss the dog.

'Hello Harvey, hello old boy, how have you been?' When he straightened up she was there, beside him. He knew he had missed her terribly but he was quite unprepared for the impact her presence had upon him. He stared at her for a long moment, at her pale shiny bobbed hair, at her clear complexion, amazingly unlined and already slightly tanned, at her round blue eyes, child-like, regarding him now with such kindness ... such love. He held out his arms and she slipped into them. For two such natural communicators, it was strange that not a single word was spoken. None was necessary.

An hour or so later, Keith emerged from the shower to find an old pair of jeans and a sweatshirt laid out on the bed. He must have left them at her cottage when he went to Australia. The relief of not having to climb back into a suit was considerable and he dressed quickly. Upstairs he found Felicity stirring something in a pot on the Aga; two wine glasses were laid out on the table. She smiled at him.

'There is some red on the side here, or some sauvignon blanc in the fridge, or a beer if you would prefer it.'

'A little white I think,' he said, 'for you too?'

She nodded. 'You must be starving,' she said. 'I presume you haven't had any lunch?'

'No,' Keith admitted. He poured the wine and held a glass out to her, returning her smile. 'What with one thing and another I forgot all about it.' They clinked glasses.

'So are you going to tell me why you're here?' Felicity asked.

The smile left his face and he sat down heavily at the table. Felicity removed her pot from the Aga and sat down beside him, taking one of his hands in hers.

'Keith, what is it?'

He took a sip of his wine. 'I'm making a fuss,' he said, 'but it did come as something of a body blow – I've been given early retirement or to put it another way, given the push.'

'What?' Felicity stared at him in disbelief. 'They can't have, not you, and what's the point, you're not far off retirement anyway?'

'The thirty-year rule,' said Keith, 'they're making sweeping redundancies in the police force across the country; anybody who has served for more than thirty years is due for culling.'

'When did you hear about it?'

'I left the meeting with my "Super" and rang you straight away.'

'I bet he's been on the force for more than thirty years,' Felicity said, furiously.

'Yes, he has,' said Keith, 'but it's different for him, he's a career policeman.'

'And you're not?'

'No, not really, I'm best down in the muck and the bullets, I'd be no good sitting in a big office planning things and playing politics – just not my style.'

'No,' said Felicity, with a smile, 'no, it's not, is it?' There was a silence between them for a moment. 'When?' she began.

'Three months, end of June.'

'It's brutal,' said Felicity, 'after all those years. What does Barbara, and the family think about it?'

'I haven't told them yet,' said Keith, 'I haven't told anybody but you. I haven't even been in touch with Jack. He must know something is up or he would have contacted me by now, he probably thinks I'm drowning my sorrows in a pub somewhere.'

'I'm glad you came to me,' said Felicity.

He looked up at her. 'Me too.'

'So what will you do?' Felicity asked.

'I've absolutely no idea. I'm not going to think about it, I've always been quite keen on denial as a way to get through most things. Tomorrow is the first day of the rest of my career and I'm going to try and find that little girl, if it's not too late, though how and where ...' His voice trailed away.

'I can't imagine ...' Felicity began and then stopped in mid sentence, 'sorry, no, I shouldn't say that.'

'Say what?' Keith asked.

She shook her head. 'It doesn't matter.' She got up and went back to the Aga.

'You were going to say you can't imagine me not being a policeman.'

She paused, hanging her head like a guilty child. 'I was, Keith, but that was a very thoughtless and stupid thing for me to say, or even think, in the current circumstances.'

'It's OK,' said Keith, 'I feel the same, but I do have three months to adjust.'

'You're a man whose cup is always half full,' Felicity said, smiling at him fondly.

'I'm struggling a bit at the moment to be my usual sunny self,' Keith replied, with a tired smile. 'It's like somebody has thrown my life up into the air and heaven knows how the pieces are going to fall.'

'I purposely haven't asked you about Australia,' Felicity said.

'And we need to talk, but can we eat first?' Keith asked. 'Whatever is in that pot, is it nearly ready?'

'It's a casserole,' said Felicity, 'and yes it is and there are some baked potatoes in the oven, will that do?'

'Perfect,' Keith replied.

During supper they kept the conversation light, talking mostly of Felicity's children and grandchildren, her work, Harvey's antics – anything but what was dominating their thoughts. It was only when the dishes were cleared away and a pot of coffee brewing that they settled down in the two Windsor chairs either side of the Aga. Their future lay like an untouched canvas before them.

'So,' Felicity said, 'how was Australia and what happened when you got back here? I didn't know what to make of the silence.'

'I am sorry,' said Keith, 'I was in such a muddle and I just felt I needed time to think things through but I should have called you, it was unforgivable.'

'So Barbara didn't come back with you?'

'No, no she is never coming back to the UK, at least not permanently. She is going to make her home out there.'

'And you?' Felicity asked, trying to keep her voice steady.

'I don't belong out there,' said Keith, 'however hard I try and despite my family settling there, I just can't imagine living in Australia permanently. If I try to look only at me the person, and exclude my relationship with you, which is obviously no easy matter, nonetheless I still believe that I would not find it easy or even possible to settle there.'

'But with your wife and daughter in Australia and one day grandchildren – what about your son, what is he going to do?'

Keith said, 'Will has found a job boat-building just outside Sydney, his long-term aim though is to start his own business. He loves the lifestyle; he is as keen as everyone else to stay.'

'And you really can't see yourself settling in, given time and now … now your career is coming to an end?' Felicity asked.

Keith shook his head. 'I just feel so out of place, it's not my home and never will be. I think the kids are still hoping that I will see sense but I honestly don't think that Barbara is really expecting me to do so.'

'Will she mind very much if you decide not to join them?' Felicity asked.

'I don't think so, not anyway for herself,' said Keith. 'Before she left, she issued me with a pretty firm ultimatum, that from now on she was going to do what suited her best, which is fair enough. Everything has always been sacrificed at the shrine of my career, I do realise that. She is staying out in Australia whatever I decide and what I do is up to me, and there is absolutely no pressure from her, and apparently no antagonism. Quite the contrary, in fact, ever since she stopped trying to make me change my ways, it's all much more relaxed. I honestly don't believe she cares what I do so long as I don't attempt to change her plans, which obviously I won't.'

'But …' said Felicity, sensing things were not that simple.

'But,' Keith agreed, 'it doesn't stop me feeling very guilty.'

'Guilty about us?' Felicity asked.

'No, I haven't got around to us yet, I'm just talking about the fact that they're over there and I am over here – it's very selfish, but I'm a Cornishman and this is where I want to end my days …' He hesitated, and then looking up at Felicity, smiled, 'and then, of course, there's you.'

'And then, of course, there's me,' said Felicity.

She got up and poured two mugs of coffee and, without asking, a brandy for Keith. She placed them on the edge of the Aga beside him and he caught her hand as she returned to her seat and pulled her down to him. She knelt beside his chair, their arms around one another.

'Here I am rambling on about myself. What about you, do you even want me hanging around in your life?'

'Yes please,' she replied, simply. They kissed deeply, then Felicity rose and returned to her chair, took a sip of coffee and regarded Keith speculatively over the top of the mug. 'I don't want to be a confusion; I don't want to be responsible for adding to the pressure you are already under. You have so much going on in your life at the moment, this decision about Australia, your career, this awful case with the missing child, I don't want you to feel you have to make any sort of decision at the moment because of me. I hated not hearing from you because I didn't know what was going on, I didn't know how to feel, but now it's alright, now I know you, well, still care about me.'

'Of course I do, I'm so sorry,' Keith said again, 'I'm so very sorry I didn't get in touch – it was crass.'

'It's OK, it's done and dusted. I think now we should just go with the flow and see what happens, but I think you should tell your family about the redundancy.'

'I will,' said Keith, 'but inevitably the kids are going to up the pressure to move out to Australia permanently. With no job, their argument will be that there is nothing to keep me here.'

'And nobody has got a clue about us, I hope?' Felicity asked.

Keith shook his head. 'I think sometimes Will has an inkling, having met you and seen us together, but I don't know. He never mentioned it while we were together in Australia.'

'We're not flavour of the month with Annie right now,' Felicity said, suddenly.

'Oh, why?' Keith asked.

'She doesn't approve.'

'How on earth does she know about us?' said Keith.

'Oh, come off it, Annie knows everything.'

'Yes, I suppose so,' Keith smiled, 'she is an amazing old girl.'

'Amazing or not, she is very disapproving of our relationship.'

'Really, that surprises me,' said Keith.

'She objects on moral grounds and of course she is right, I shouldn't be spending time with a man who isn't mine.'

'She is a big chapel-goer, isn't she?' Keith said.

'Nothing wrong with that.'

'No, I agree, but it explains her feelings on the subject.'

'Do you think she has a point?' Felicity asked.

'I go round and round it in my head,' Keith said, 'but I can't believe that what is happening here, to us, is wrong.'

'Nor me,' Felicity said quietly, 'nor me.'

The following morning Keith slipped out of the bed while Felicity still slept, showered, dressed hurriedly and calling softly to Harvey, clipped on a lead and headed out of the door towards the harbour beach. The wind had dropped, it was a still, beautiful morning, a smattering of dog walkers were already about, the tide was way out. Keith felt calmer than he had done in days, probably weeks, he thought. He had not felt settled like this since he was last in St Ives with Felicity. He felt grounded, confident that he and this woman whom he loved so much would make the right decision in the end for everyone. He knew how lucky he was to have this unconditional love and he knew it was important not to take advantage of it. Ever since he had left Felicity and travelled to Australia, he had felt disconnected, rootless and that in turn had sapped his confidence and sense of well-being. Now he felt centred again, felt a sense of belonging and in turn it meant he could get back to work, to concentrate properly.

At the end of the harbour beach he whistled to Harvey and climbed up the steps by the pier, weaved his way past the museum, down the steps to the Porthgwidden car park, heading for Porthgwidden beach and the Island. Harvey raced ahead of him, confident in this familiar route around the town. Having walked a circuit of the Island, Keith sat down on a bench overlooking Porthmeor beach. Although it was very early and the tide was well out, there were a number of surfers already enjoying a good swell. He gazed at them and then out beyond the beach to the craggy outline of Man's Head. It was good to be back in St Ives. If he was to settle anywhere, this would be as good a place as any, better than most, best of all perhaps.

His thoughts turned to Fiona McAllister. Where was she, was the poor little thing even still alive? There had to be a link between the two cases even though it made no sense. Graham had assured him that not a stone had been left unturned in trying to seek a connection between the two families, but something had been overlooked, it was the only way to make any sense of this double murder. He would ask permission to go and re-interview Ian McAllister. Maybe he could find a connection, there had to be one, there just had to be one.

6

Felicity sat at her desk and stared at the half-finished illustration before her. The subject was a forlorn baby seal who had lost its mother and was swimming a little way off shore looking anxiously at a small boy paddling in the shallows who was destined to be his friend. It was a charming children's story and Felicity had set about the task of illustrating it with great enthusiasm, but this morning she found she just could not concentrate. Keith had left an hour earlier to go to work with the promise of returning in the evening. They had been back together for less than twenty-four hours, such a short time, and yet the impact of his return into her life was enormous, overwhelming. Her commitment to him, she knew, was total, yet whether they had a future together or not still seemed uncertain. He had too much going on to think clearly – an emotive case to solve, impending retirement and the big one, whether to return to his family. She knew she must make no demands on him herself, it wasn't fair. Whatever decision he made, it had to be made alone and all she could do was wait. Always a proactive person, inclined to spontaneous and occasionally ill-judged actions, Felicity's mind rebelled against the concept of hanging around, waiting for something to happen but she could really see no alternative. If she loved him, and she certainly did, then this was how it was going to have to be.

It was just so hard. She thought back to her early days with her husband, Charlie. Had she loved Charlie more than she now loved Keith? She thought not. Ridiculous as it was, now the wrong side of fifty, her feelings for Keith were as strong and as true as hers had ever been for her husband. Yet of course it was difficult to disentangle her feelings in the early days of marriage from the life she had subsequently lived with Charlie. They had been largely happy, very happy in many respects – they shared two children and a life together in Oxford which at the time had fulfilled them both, but now seemed utterly remote.

By contrast, her feelings for Keith were surprisingly simplistic in what was a complex situation. Maybe age had matured her, although she had always considered, almost hoped, it had not. Maybe there is less 'me, me, me' in this relationship than there would have been when the young

Felicity met Charlie Paradise. Certainly she could not imagine exercising the patience now required of her. 'Never weigh love,' she suddenly remembered her mother saying to her, 'you love different people in different ways; you will love your children differently because they are different.' As soon as the thought came into her mind, an image suddenly came back to Felicity of her mother sitting at the kitchen table in Oxford, Jamie was a toddler and she was expecting Mel. She had asked her mother whether she would be able to love this second child as much as she loved the first and that had been the reply. How true it had been; her children were so very different and she did indeed love them differently. To try to make comparisons between Charlie and Keith was pointless; two very different men, yet oddly, Felicity thought suddenly, they would have liked each other.

The phone rang, making her jump. She lifted the receiver with some relief to escape her feelings. It was Martin. 'Hi Fizzy, I was wondering if you would like to join Charlie and me for lunch at the Bluff Inn today. We're at a bit of a loose end, I'm on babysitting duty, Minty's at school and Mel is going to be late back from work. Charlie is cutting a tooth, he is very grumpy and we are already pretty hacked off with one another. I'm slightly hoping Granny might keep the peace. Anyway, it would be nice to see you.'

'I'd love that, Martin, shall I see you there?'

'Yes, twelvish, Charlie likes his lunch early as you know and we could walk Harvey on the beach afterwards.'

'Perfect,' said Felicity.

Keith Penrose was also finding it difficult to concentrate on work; his mind was full of Felicity. It was ridiculous at his age to be mooning around like some besotted teenager, yet he was grateful for the distraction. On his way into the station, several of his junior officers had greeted him but avoided eye contact, so everyone must know he had been laid off. Jack was out. There had been a number of thefts around the farms of West Cornwall, big thefts too – an entire barn of winter feed, a quad bike, a flock of sheep, tools and now, most recently, he was told a John Deere tractor. Both Keith and Jack were farmer's sons, it was one of the many things they had in common. They knew how hard it was to make a living off the land and Keith completely understood why Jack was so incensed by this spate of burglaries which had been going on for months now and which had provided precious few clues. Whoever they were, these guys were good.

He sat behind his still unnaturally tidy desk with a revolting cup of coffee, staring down at the notes he had made. Ed McAllister, two years old; who in God's name would kill a two-year-old? Decision made, he lifted the receiver and dialled Graham Sinclair's number.

'Graham,' he said, 'you say we still have some blood-stained clothes from the Johnson murder, we probably even have both Katie Johnson and her mother's blood samples knocking around still, I imagine. Could you run a DNA match on their blood samples with those of the McAllister family, mother and son and the father too, come to that.'

'There is no point, Keith,' Graham said, 'there is absolutely no connection between the two families.'

Keith gave a heavy sigh. 'Humour me, would you, Graham, and just organise it. I can't understand why it hasn't been done already. DNA is normally the first port of call for cold cases these days.'

'I'm not sure anyone is going to be too pleased about this, Keith, there's just no point. If there was a link we would have found it.'

'Look,' said Keith, rapidly losing his temper, 'you drag me up to London to help you with this case, you're getting nowhere and as every day goes by, the chances of finding Fiona alive are fading. There is very little point in consulting me unless you are going to take notice of what I have to say. I don't want to pull rank here, Graham, but I'm telling you, not asking you, to run those tests and if anyone higher up doesn't like it, tell them to get on to me ... and I'd like them done fast.'

'OK, OK,' said Graham, 'there is no need to lose your rag, Keith, I'll get on with it now but why, what makes you think there is any point?'

'Just put it down to a hunch,' said Keith, dismissively.

The Bluff Inn at Hayle is very much geared to tourists – a huge bar, the sort of cheap, cheerful food which the visitors like and a massive garden area outside overlooking the Hayle estuary. There was no wind and although the air had a March chilliness to it, the sun was high in the sky so they had decided to sit outside. A portion of fish with the occasional chip to suck on soon sorted out Charlie. He was a young man whose humour was always improved by food and lots of it.

Felicity was extremely fond of her son-in-law and she knew the feeling was reciprocated. They had become firm friends before Mel had even met Martin. Martin's first wife had been tragically killed in a car accident, very much around the same time as Charlie had died. The loss of their respective spouses had created a bond – that and the fact that Martin was nearer in age to his wife's mother than to his wife. They chatted idly while Charlie was fed, then they put him on a rug on the grass by their feet with some toys and Harvey to entertain him.

'I might as well tell you,' said Martin, without preamble, 'the jungle drums are beating in the family. Everyone is worried about you.'

'Good heavens, why?' Felicity asked, genuinely confused.

'Well, it's about you and your inspector, isn't it,' said Martin.

'So this lunch is a set-up?' Felicity asked, playing for time, while her mind raced as to what to say.

'No, no, it's my own initiative. Neither of your children are going to tackle you on the subject, at least not at the moment, so I thought I'd wade in and see if there is anything I can do to help.'

'Why do you think I need help?' Felicity asked.

'Ever since Keith went off to Australia you've been as miserable as sin and now he is back, Mel gets the impression that you two haven't seen one another. It's none of my business,' Martin added, 'so tell me to get stuffed, but I don't like seeing you unhappy.' Felicity stared at Martin's handsome, anxious face and felt a rush of warmth towards him. He was such a thoroughly decent man, Mel was very lucky to have found him. A slight altercation on the rug interrupted them, concerning a ball which both Charlie and Harvey felt they owned. Having sorted out the dispute, Martin returned to his seat. If Felicity was hoping the subject might be changed, she was sadly mistaken. 'Well?' said Martin.

'I saw Keith yesterday,' said Felicity, 'everything is fine and I'm sorry I've been grumpy, I didn't mean to be.'

'Is that all I'm going to get?' Martin asked.

'I think so,' Felicity replied, carefully.

'Look, I'm treading on thin ice here, I know, but I'm aware that you are very fond of Keith and he of you and I'm also aware that he is married. I just don't want to see you hurt, none of us do.'

'I know,' said Felicity, putting a hand on his arm, 'and I really appreciate your kindness, but I'm fine. I am extremely grown up and I really can work this out for myself.'

'OK,' said Martin, 'subject closed, other than to say that if ever you do need to talk about it and you find it easier to talk to me rather than your children, then you won't hesitate to give me a shout, will you?'

Felicity smiled at him. 'Thank you Martin, it is very kind of you and I will remember what you say but I am fine, absolutely fine.'

Jack Curnow tumbled into Keith's office mid-morning, flushed and angry. 'Another tractor,' he said, 'a nearly new John Deere, how can it possibly disappear off the face of the earth? It's not exactly inconspicuous is it? The poor guy just shelled out

£95,000 for it.'

'Presumably he's insured?' Keith asked.

'Yes, but there's a huge excess and anyway that's not the point, he's been longing for this tractor for years. Finally he got it, only had it for three weeks and now it's stolen and we seem unable to do anything about it. I'm sorry, it's so frustrating.'

'It's OK,' said Keith, amused and gratified by Jack's passion.

An appalled expression suddenly crossed Jack Curnow's face. 'Sir, there's a rumour circulating ...'

'And it's true,' said Keith, grimly. 'I've got three months.'

'They have to be off their heads, why you?'

'The thirty-year rule has been well and truly exceeded.'

Jack's anger drained away. 'I'm really sorry.'

Keith met his eye. 'Me too, I can't even imagine not being here doing this job.' They sat in silence for a moment. 'Still,' said Keith, 'we've got three months, let's show them, shall we, Jack? Let's show them just how good we are.'

'Are you getting anywhere with the McAllister murders?' Jack asked.

Keith shook his head. 'About as much progress as you with the farm thefts.'

'Well, sir,' said Jack, 'I suppose the only way we can go from here, then, is up.'

7

May Farrell and her dog Jem, a collie/German shepherd cross, toiled up the hill out of Nancledra and took the left hand turning to Towednack which would lead them home. Well into her sixties now, May had walked further than she had meant to do. Yesterday there had been a real sense of spring in the air, but today it seemed that winter was back; it was grey and overcast and a nasty little south-westerly was making it feel very chill. She hoped her husband Tom had remembered to light the fire. His circulation had always been better than hers; a life of farming, out in all weathers, always on the go, a lean spare man full of energy, he never seemed to feel the cold. A fresh flurry of wind made her shiver.

It was because of the wind that she didn't hear the lorry at first, there was so little traffic on this road, even in the season. When she did spot it, it was coming hurtling down the lane out of the gloom of the afternoon with no headlights. Jem, an obedient dog, who had never been on a lead in his long life, was walking right into the path of the lorry which seemed to be travelling at such speed as to be almost out of control.

'Jem, Jem!' May shouted, but the old dog was getting deaf and didn't appear to hear her. She rushed towards him, pushing him out of the way and in doing so placed herself directly in the path of the oncoming lorry.

It was over an hour before May's neighbour, Jerry Spencer, drove down the lane with his daughter to take her to work in one of the restaurants in St Ives. They stopped just short of the body. As they rushed towards it, they recognised it immediately as being that of May. Jem, who was sitting beside his mistress, began to growl, teeth bared – he was not going to let them anywhere near her. In the end it was her husband, Tom, who had to coax his dog away so that his wife could be taken to the mortuary.

Felicity had made a fish pie which Keith ate with some relish, having inevitably missed lunch. After supper they walked Harvey around the Island and returned to the cottage for a glass of wine in front of the Aga.

'This isn't very fair on you, is it?' Keith said after a while.

'How do you mean?' Felicity asked.

'This sort of state of limbo, I need to say something to you, to Barbara, make a statement of intent I suppose.'

'Are you genuinely ready to do that?' Felicity asked.

'I feel I should,' said Keith.

'I don't really think that's the same thing and I'm absolutely certain you shouldn't rush into it. Whatever the decision, once made, it can't be changed.'

'I can't ever leave you,' Keith said.

'And I don't want you to,' said Felicity, smiling at him a little sadly, 'but let's just wait a while. We're alright as we are, aren't we?'

'Yes, of course we are,' said Keith.

'Well then,' Felicity said, 'as my eldest grandson would say, chill, just chill, Chief Inspector.'

As if on cue Keith's mobile rang.

'Calm down,' Felicity heard him say, 'calm down Jack, just start again and tell me exactly what happened.' There was a long silence while Keith listened intently then he spoke. 'Actually, Jack, I'm in St Ives at the moment, it won't take me long to join you, so give me the directions ... I take the Towednack road just before Nancledra, yes, yes I know it. I'll be there in ten, fifteen minutes at the outside.' Keith switched off his mobile and stood up, looking apologetically at Felicity. 'I'm sorry but I'll have to go, there's been a nasty hit and run at Towednack. We've had a lot of thefts of farm equipment and stock recently but this time they seemed to have killed someone in the process of stealing a herd of prize Herefords.'

'God, how awful,' said Felicity. She smiled at him slightly shyly. 'So what is the protocol, do I sit up and wait for you or do I go to bed and wait for you?'

Keith grinned. 'Definitely bed and wait for me,' he said slipping his arms around her and lifting her up so that she was enclosed in the circle of his arms. They kissed. 'Now look, that's quite enough,' said Keith drawing away, 'this is no way to send a man off to work, you baggage.'

She smiled at him. 'This is weird,' she said, 'it feels almost kind of domestic.'

Keith considered her words as he strode up the hill towards Barnoon car park. He wasn't behaving well, he realised. How could he have put them, as Felicity described it, into a domestic situation when he hadn't even told his wife he was being forced into early retirement – let alone that he was planning to stay in Cornwall and that there was a new woman in his life. The degree of moral cowardice was appalling. The words from Hamlet,

Polonius's advice to his son came suddenly to him: 'to thine own self be true, and it must follow as the night the day, thou canst not then be false to any man.' Well, he wasn't being true to himself, he was behaving badly and he needed to sort it out, and soon. He reached his car and drove down the hill towards Stennack. Then his mind cleared and all his concentration was focused on the job ahead.

Keith found Jack Curnow sitting beside the Rayburn in a farmhouse kitchen which in most people's eyes would be the perfect epitome of how a farmhouse kitchen should look: drying herbs and onions, a persistent smell of baking, gleaming pots, shining pottery, a handsome dresser on which a tabby cat lay curled up, and a huge kitchen table scrubbed within an inch of its life but bearing the scars of many years of service. This was where the comfort ended. Sitting in a chair opposite Jack was what Keith assumed would be normally an elderly but strong, vigorous man. Now he was reduced to a crumpled heap. He wasn't crying, it was worse than that, his features seemed to have slipped, he was lost in himself. By his side a dog sat pressed to his knees, half-sitting on his feet and trembling violently. The trembling seemed to permeate the old man's body so it looked as if they were both shivering in unison, it was a pitiful sight.

Jack got to his feet. 'This is Tom Farrell, sir.'

Tom looked up, acknowledged Keith with a nod and returned to gazing at the floor with apparently unseeing eyes.

'So tell me exactly what happened here,' Keith said.

'Tom has a herd of prize Herefords. He frequently picks up prizes at all the shows around – obviously Royal Cornwall, but shows up-country too. He is a renowned breeder. The cattle lorry must have arrived just as it was getting dark this evening, Tom's helper had gone home and his wife was out walking the dog. Because it was a miserable night, Tom had come inside and was working on the accounts. Presumably the villains saw that the light was on in the farmhouse and assumed, or knew, that they would not be disturbed. They loaded the cattle lorry with as many beasts as they could get in, by the looks of it.'

'How many?' Keith asked.

'At least thirty,' Tom murmured, his voice sounded reedy and thin.

Jack gave a great sigh, stood up and began ranging around the room. 'They obviously left in a great hurry, sir. They were driving out of Towednack back towards the main road and May, Tom's wife, and her dog were in the way. The dog was OK but they struck May and just drove on.'

'And how do we know that it was the cattle lorry which hit May?' Keith asked.

'Because, young fellow,' Tom said, 'they made such a mess of my May that it couldn't have been anything but a big vehicle and anyway my neighbour saw a cattle lorry going at fantastic speed heading out towards the A30.'

'We've put out an alert?' Keith began.

'Yes, of course we have, sir,' said Jack impatiently, 'but there's no sign of the lorry yet.'

'It's no consolation at all to you, Mr Farrell, I appreciate that,' said Keith, 'but rest assured we will find that lorry and link it to your wife's death.' The old man nodded curtly. 'Would it be possible to see where the cattle were taken from?' Keith asked, more to get Jack out of the room than anything else.

'The lad will show you where,' the old man murmured.

The two men hesitated and then wordlessly opened the kitchen door and stepped outside.

'What on earth is the point of inspecting the field?' Jack said angrily, 'there's nothing to see anyway and it's pitch dark out here.'

'I appreciate that,' said Keith calmly, 'but I felt we were not helping Tom Farrell or ourselves, come to that, by hanging around. He needs to be alone and he certainly could do without a couple of idiots like us cluttering up his kitchen, particularly not you – I can see how deeply this has affected you.'

'I told you,' Jack said, 'I told you this was getting out of hand.'

'What do you mean?' Keith asked, frowning at him.

'These farm thefts, they've been getting bigger and bigger, more confident, taking more risks, reckless ... and now this death – that poor couple.'

'They remind you of your mum and dad, don't they?' Keith said, shrewdly.

Jack nodded. 'The kitchen, it was like being at home.'

'I know what you mean.' Keith put a hand on Jack's shoulder. 'Come on, show me around the farm.'

It was after midnight when Keith let himself into Jericho Cottage. Felicity had taken herself off to bed as instructed and was sitting up reading.

'How was it?' she asked.

'Awful,' Keith said, 'hang on a moment, I've been tramping around a farmyard, I'll just go and shower and then I'll be with you.'

Minutes later he joined her. 'Jack is mad at me and rightly so,' Keith said.

'Why?'

'He feels I should have been taking these farm

thefts more seriously. A cattle lorry mowed down and killed a lovely woman this evening, and in the process destroyed her husband, as well. Ironically the villains were making their escape having just loaded the family's prize herd into the back of their lorry, a double whammy if you like – awful. Anyway, enough of all that, how have you been?'

Felicity put down her book. 'Missing you,' she said, 'pathetic, isn't it?'

Keith slipped an arm around her and drew her close. 'Completely pathetic. Incidentally, I think Jack might be starting to smell a rat.'

'Really, does it matter?'

'I don't think so, no. I have kept very few secrets from him over the years, and he is very discreet. He's also no fool and it was fairly obvious that I wasn't going back to Truro tonight but returning to St Ives.'

Later as they lay in the dark in one another's arms, Felicity said 'A funny thing happened this evening when I was walking Harvey just before bedtime.'

'What sort of thing?' said Keith, hovering on the verge of sleep.

'I felt I was being followed.'

Keith's eyes snapped open. 'How do you mean?'

'Well, it was ridiculous really, it was just a

feeling. I came out of the cottage, I never normally lock the door as you know, and Harvey and I went down to the harbour but I had this kind of feeling that someone was behind me and Harvey was nervous too, he was anxious to stay close to me.'

'And did anything happen?'

'No, not exactly, we went round the Island as normal but when I got back to the cottage, it felt as if someone had been in here.'

Keith was very alert now. 'So had anything been moved or taken?'

'No, nothing like that, it was just a feeling and when I shut the door Harvey's hackles went up, he felt it too.'

'So that is why the door was locked when I arrived home tonight. I thought you were being unusually sensible. Do you think you and Harvey may have had an overdose of imagination?'

'Probably,' said Felicity, anxious not to add to his burdens. 'The town is so quiet at the moment it is easy to imagine things in the shadows.' She felt Keith relax against her, pleased that she had calmed his anxiety – but she had not calmed her own.

8

Keith sat at his desk eyeing the telephone suspiciously. The previous day he had e-mailed Barbara and suggested that she ring him at the office on the landline around five. It was now five-forty and there had been no call from her. For some reason he could not quite fathom, he was reluctant to go home and call her from there. He knew he needed to go back to fetch some clean clothes, if nothing else, but the thought of returning to the old family home felt increasingly awkward. He decided he would give it until six o'clock and if Barbara hadn't rung by then he would go home and make the call. The thought of speaking to Barbara was nerve-racking, not least because he had no plan. He would tell her about his redundancy and see how she reacted. That was as far as he had got in his thinking.

He tried to re-focus his mind on work. They had found the cattle lorry which he was sure tests would reveal was the vehicle which had killed May Farrell, There were obvious signs of trauma and bloodstains on the radiator. The cattle had gone of course and so had the villains. The vehicle had been simply abandoned in a lay-by just the other side of Bodmin. Jack was beside himself with frustration and Keith, now they were dealing with a murder enquiry, was equally enraged. All the farmers who had been the victims of previous thefts had been re-interviewed, looking again for clues, anything that would help them identify the thieves but they seemed to be too good at what they did – they arrived, caused chaos and now a death, and disappeared into the night – it was frustrating to say the least, to be able to get away with the theft of so many cattle and to manage to change vehicles without being spotted.

The phone rang, interrupting his thoughts. He stared at it and then with a sinking heart picked it up. 'Barbara?' he said.

'No, Graham here, Keith, Graham Sinclair.'

A wave of cowardly relief swept over Keith. 'Graham, what news?'

'Startling,' said Graham, 'to say the least. Can you come up to the Yard? We really need you here, now. Is there a train you could catch tonight?'

'I could catch the sleeper,' said Keith, 'which would get me into your office at say, eight-thirty to nine tomorrow morning, would that do?'

'Yes, that would do. You do live in a damnably inconvenient part of the world, Keith.'

'Well, I'm sorry about that,' said Keith.

'Right well, we'll see you in the morning then.'

'Hang on,' said Keith, 'you can't expect me to drop everything and come up to London without telling me what's going on. I have a murder enquiry going on down here, too.'

'I'd rather give you the whole picture when you arrive.'

'Something,' said Keith, 'give me something if you want me to come.'

'I can't give you something without giving you everything. Still,' said Graham, brightening, 'I suppose a long train journey provides good thinking time.'

'That it certainly does,' said Keith, 'so spill the beans.'

'You were right,' said Graham, 'it was worth doing a DNA test but the results are extraordinary, to say the least.'

'Go on,' said Keith, sobering instantly.

'Katie Johnson.'

'Yes,' said Keith.

'Katie Johnson's the child who ...'

'I know who Katie Johnson is,' said Keith, 'Katie Johnson is the twin who died at the scene.'

'Katie Johnson had a twin sister,' said Graham.

'I know that,' said Keith impatiently, 'Janey. I've spent half my life, more than half my life, thinking about Janey.'

Graham ignored him. 'Katie Johnson had a twin sister, her twin sister is Moira McAllister, the mother ...'

'The mother of Fiona?' Keith finished for him.

'Exactly and while you'll still reeling from that, Keith, Katie Johnson and her twin sister were not the natural children of Caroline Johnson who also died at the scene. There is no DNA match of any sort – they are simply unrelated.'

There was a very long silence while Keith digested the information that he had been given. 'So what you are saying is that Janey Johnson is, was, Moira McAllister? She disappeared and then turns up as a murder victim like her sister forty years later.'

'Yes, that's about it,' said Graham, 'We've found Janey, it's taken a while and when we did find her she was dead. We have yet to establish what happened to her on the night of the fourteenth of October 1970 but at least we know what she became.'

Keith frowned. 'If Moira McAllister is Janey Johnson, isn't she rather old to have a two-year-old?'

'Yes,' Graham agreed, 'she was forty-six. She and Ian McAllister married late, they had difficulty conceiving so they had IVF. Both babies, Fiona and Ed, were conceived that way. Forty-four is not a great age these days to have a child. It is quite often difficult to conceive but once the baby is established there is usually no difficulty in proceeding to birth.'

'I hadn't realised you were an expert,' Keith said, dryly.

'My wife is an obstetrician so I know a bit about it.'

There was a long silence between the two men again.

'So,' said Keith at last, 'if this is some kind of strange vendetta against this family, if the pattern is being repeated, there is a chance Fiona McAllister could still be alive?'

'My thoughts exactly,' said Graham, 'which is one of the reasons we want you up here double quick.'

'We need to get hold of Thomas Johnson,' Keith said after a moment. 'You said, I think, that you believed him to be still alive.'

'Yes he is, he lives in an apartment in Washington DC and that's one of the things we want you to do, Keith. You were the one who had a relationship with him when the original tragedy happened. We would like you to go to Washington and interview him. Among other things, he is probably the only person who can tell us why his wife wasn't the biological mother to his children.'

'Right,' said Keith, 'so I'd better go and pack a bag then and find my passport.'

'That's about it,' said Graham.

'Anything else?' Keith said, airily.

'Umm, yes,' said Graham. 'Good work, Keith. DNA was the obvious way to go but having established that there was no obvious link between the two families, we hadn't pursued it. Congratulations, you were right.'

'OK, there's is no need to go overboard,' said Keith, 'but if I am to go to Washington I need to know everything, I have to be properly briefed and in future if I want to pursue a line of enquiry, I don't expect to have to beg.'

'Fair comment,' said Graham, 'I'll see you in the morning.'

For a long moment after replacing the receiver, Keith sat still as a statue. Then he was galvanised into action. He jumped up and scribbled a note to Jack telling him where he would be in the next few days and then hurried down to the car park. He drove straight back home without a qualm now and after a frantic search for his passport, found it and began packing a bag. There was no time to call Barbara now, he thought with relief. Only as he packed did the enormity of what had just happened hit him. For forty years he had been plagued by the image of Katie Johnson lying dead beside her mother and of Janey Johnson who he had never been able to find. Now, suddenly it was clear that Janey had lived a life – she had grown up, married, had children ... the fleeting euphoria left him – and then had died, as her sister had died, alongside her little son. What was going on? If the person who had killed the Johnsons had preserved the life of Janey, surely he could not have been the same person who had gone on to kill her when she was a mature woman in her forties. Suddenly a thought struck Keith and searching for his mobile phone on the bed amongst all his scattered shirts, he rang Graham Sinclair.

'You are going for an absolute news blackout on this development, aren't you?'

'Yes, yes,' said Graham, 'we don't intend telling the public more than we need to at this stage.'

'I'm deadly serious,' said Keith, 'think about it. We don't understand what is going on yet but we know now that the murders are linked. As we discussed, the pattern, if it is being repeated, suggests that at this moment Fiona McAllister is alive, but she may only be alive because the killer thinks we have not made the connection that she is Janey Johnson's daughter. If we go blabbing to the public that there is a connection, who knows what might happen?'

'I think the key to this could be the identity of the biological mother of these girls. The link has to be there and maybe the explanation as to what has happened. You can rely on a news blackout up here, and I don't have to ask the same of you, do I? Discuss the case with no one.' Graham's tone irritated Keith but he did not rise to the bait. However, it was with a heavy heart, that he rang Felicity a few minutes later and explained there had been a development with the McAllister case and he had to take the sleeper to London and that he might be called upon to go to Washington.

'What's happened?' Felicity asked, her natural curiosity overtaking any form of discretion.

'I don't know yet,' Keith said, hating himself for lying and longing to share the news with her.

'Well, take care, my love,' she said, 'and let me know if you're going to cross the pond.'

'I will, and you look after yourself – no more stalking or bumps in the night, I hope?'

'No,' Felicity said, 'it was probably just my over-developed sense of the dramatic, which you know so well.'

'I certainly do.'

'I love you, Chief Inspector.'

'I love you too, Mrs Paradise.'

9

Felicity was feeling forlorn. She had put a brave face on it when talking to Keith about his departure to London and from there to Washington, but in reality she was feeling bereft. She realised now that her life had been on hold since Keith had left for Australia. She had gone about her normal tasks of work and looking after her grandchildren but in reality she had been in a state of limbo and from what Martin had said, a pretty disgruntled and miserable state of limbo at that. Keith's arrival back in her life had been wonderful but, with the future still so uncertain, she felt restless and nervy which was not like her normal self. 'Bloody men,' she thought as she stood on her balcony looking out towards the harbour, were they worth it?

The fog of misery that had followed Charlie's death had cleared and the years in between then and now had been content, fulfilled even. Admittedly, running through them had been the frisson of her budding relationship with Keith, but until now it had only been a part of her life. Now it seemed to be all-consuming. Instead of being her own person, she suddenly felt she was half of a whole once more. It was not a bad feeling so long as the other half was stable, which clearly was not the case at the moment.

'Drat it,' she said to herself aloud and dug into her jeans pocket for her mobile. She needed to do something, something for herself instead of moping around waiting for Keith to return. She scrolled down her address book until she found the name Ellie. Ellie was Felicity's god-daughter and, since Ellie's mother had died, a great deal more – a proxy daughter really. Ellie's mother, Gilla, had been Felicity's best friend since childhood and her death had deepened the already close bond between Ellie and Felicity. When it was discovered that Ellie's biological father was Josh Buchanan, who was not only a close friend but had also been Charlie's junior partner in his law firm, Josh and Felicity had joined forces to become unofficial parents to Ellie.

Ellie had finished university now, the family home had been sold and she had bought herself a little house in Oxford, renting out one room to a friend from her schooldays. She had a good job at the Oxford University Press and her mind set on a career in publishing. Curiously, despite some difficult years, Ellie had become a more stable, well-adjusted and sensible person than either of her biological parents. Her mother, Gilla, had been a clever woman, marvellously good-looking, but she had trivialised her life. She could have been anything she wanted to be but instead she had run a gift shop in Woodstock – admittedly with flair, but hardly intellectually stimulating. Her hobby was men and a number of ill-advised affairs had caused a lot of trouble during her life. Josh Buchanan, by contrast, had been born with a silver spoon – rich, good-looking and idle, he too had taken the easy road. He read law because his father suggested he should and having joined Charlie in his Oxford law practice, spent many happy years seducing good-looking undergraduates; when he became too old for that, he turned his attention to the bored yummy mummies of North Oxford with too much time on their hands. He had never married because that would have involved too much commitment. It was therefore touching to see now that at well past fifty, and having discovered that he had a daughter, he was starting to think about someone other than himself.

Ellie answered the phone on the second ring.

'Fizzy, how are you? I've been meaning to ring you for weeks and weeks – in fact it is positively creepy because Josh and I were only talking about you last night.'

Felicity was gratified. She didn't deserve to be thought about, she had been so useless to her friends of late. 'I'm so sorry for not having been in touch,' she began.

'Say no more,' said Ellie. 'Look, we had this idea. We're both free this coming weekend. How would it be if we came down to St Ives to see you, just for the weekend? We won't overstay our welcome.'

'That would be great,' said Felicity and meant it. There was no way Keith would be back until early next week. 'The trouble is I've only got one spare room, as you know.'

'We thought of that,' said Ellie, 'Josh is going to book into a B and B or perhaps you could find one for him, something in town close to you. He said it would be good if I could stay with you so that we can have girl talks.'

'Good heavens,' said Felicity, 'I feel quite flattered. I can't imagine he really thinks that someone in their fifties could manage much girl talk with a young woman in her twenties.'

'I think he imagines we are going to talk about Mum,' said Ellie, gently.

At the mention of Gilla, an image of her flashed into Felicity's mind – the bright red curls, the mad laugh, the glass of wine raised in a toast. She imagined Ellie having much the same thoughts.

'That would be great,' she said, chastened. 'I'll find a B and B suitable for Josh. When will you arrive?'

'Friday in time for supper,' said Ellie, 'but don't cook, book us somewhere nice to eat out, our treat.'

Felicity thought about her god-daughter when she finished the phone call, marvelling at her resilience. She was now an extremely wealthy young woman. Her father in name, Gilla's husband, having been a banker, had amassed a considerable sum of money over the years, but it had not gone to Ellie's head. All she needed now was a decent man in her life, which of course in turn reminded Felicity of the decent man in her own – what was he doing, where was he? How she missed him already.

The man in question had just booked himself into the usual dreary hotel round the corner from New Scotland Yard. He was also booked on an early flight to Washington the following morning. He had spent the day debriefing everyone he could on the subject of the McAllister/Johnson case. There was a new respect, he observed with amusement, in the Met's dealings with him, and so there should be, he thought. It was ridiculous that no one had thought to check out the DNA of both families, but then that was the advantage of bringing someone in from outside to look at things with fresh eyes. He wondered if there would be any role for him once he had retired: maybe taking a fresh look at cold cases. He smiled to himself as he took the evil-smelling rickety lift up to his bedroom; there was a long tradition of eccentric private sleuths – Miss Marple, Poirot, Sherlock Holmes – was it a requirement to be slightly odd to be successful in such a career? The thought suddenly depressed him – not being part of the team after all these years – and as he unlocked the door to his bedroom he put the idea firmly out of his mind. Concentrating on the here and now is what he had to do, for Fiona's sake.

Following an indifferent supper in the restaurant, he rang Felicity and was glad to hear she had her god-daughter coming for the weekend. She sounded chirpy, which made him miss her more and emphasised the need to ring Barbara, but he couldn't cope with it now, his head was too full of the interview ahead with Thomas Johnson. With the aid of the Washington police, it had been established that Johnson was alive and well and currently living in an apartment in central Washington, not far from the White House. He had been retired for a couple of years, he had never remarried and lived alone as far as anyone could tell. It had been decided that the element of surprise would be important and so, having established that Keith was not travelling to Washington on a wild goose chase, Thomas Johnson had been given no prior warning of the interview.

Having been round the facts again and again, Keith's tired mind could still make little sense of it. Moira McAllister had been Janey Johnson – of that there could be no doubt, the DNA was an identical match – so how come she had a different name, had lived to be a middle-aged woman and then suffered the same fate as her sister; and why was Caroline Johnson not their mother? It was not an unusual scenario for DNA tests to reveal that the man the children thought of as their father was not their father at all, but it was unusual for the same thing to apply to the mother. How had Thomas and Caroline Johnson acquired the girls then? They were not adopted. One of Keith's tasks was to obtain a DNA sample from Thomas Johnson. Assuming he was the father then who on earth was the mother?

Moira's husband, Ian, seemed as baffled as the Met as to the identity of his wife. Keith had not met him but had listened to the recorded interview. The couple had not met until they were into their late thirties, both having been dedicated to their careers in their early lives; at least that is what Ian had suggested. Ian headed up a sizeable pharmaceutical business and Moira was marketing director for a group of health food shops which had expanded throughout London and was now conquering the provinces. Since Ed was born she had only worked three days a week, but apparently loved her job.

They had met initially at a dinner party at a friend's house; the friend, Shirley, worked with Moira and Shirley's husband, Robert, worked for Ian. As Ian said in his interview, he suspected that their friends had actively plotted some matchmaking and it had worked – worked fantastically well. There had been a pause in the tape during which the poor man had broken down. He was clearly genuine – apart from the fact his alibi was cast iron, his obvious devotion to his wife and family was there for all to see.

Shirley and Robert Preston had also been interviewed but Moira's past seemed to be not so much a closed book as a blank sheet, so far as both her husband and her friends were aware. Ostensibly, she had posed as an only child whose parents were dead. She had studied history at Durham University and achieved a perfectly respectable 2:1. After a couple of false starts she had landed the job with the health food store when it was still just that, one store, and her career had grown with the business.

The Met had been unable to find a single friend who had known Moira since childhood; most strange of all was that while she had existed in the present with a passport and national insurance number and, of course, a marriage certificate, no record could be found of a birth certificate, although presumably one must have been available at the time of her marriage. Moira appeared to be a person with no past, which in turn underlined the indisputable fact that she had been born Janey Johnson.

10

The cab took Keith straight from the airport to the address he had been given for Thomas Johnson. It was a very smart apartment building, what Keith supposed you would call a service flat in the UK. There was an awning out over the street, carpeted steps led up through swing doors to a concierge dressed up to the nines, smiling a welcome to visitors. Keith asked if Thomas Johnson was in and was relieved to hear that he was.

'Shall I call him up, sir, and see if he is able to receive you?'

Keith resisted the temptation to flash his badge and say Thomas Johnson would see him whether he wanted to or not; that was not the way to start the interview. He simply smiled sweetly and waited while the concierge rang the number and gave Keith's name.

'He says go on right up sir, second floor, flat 14, turn right out of the elevator.'

'Thanks,' said Keith. So what would Thomas

Johnson be thinking in the time it took Keith to reach his door, would he even remember the name? Keith had only been a sergeant at the time, it was DI Lewisham that he would probably remember best as the man who had failed to find his wife's and daughter's killer. He felt very unsure of his welcome.

He need not have worried. He had barely reached the door of number 14 when it was flung open. An elderly stooped man stood in the doorway; he was virtually bald with a wrinkled craggy face but his eyes shone with intelligence and interest.

'My God, Keith Penrose, I don't believe it. Apart from the odd grey hair you've hardly changed at all.'

Keith extended his hand. 'Mr Johnson, I didn't expect you to remember me.'

'Of course I remember you, come in, come in.'

The apartment was clearly expensively furnished and to Keith's untutored eye, the paintings on the wall, mostly of seascapes, looked original. Although it was only midday, it was dull outside and the lamps in the apartment were all lit, giving a cosy glow, a welcoming feel. Thomas Johnson waved him to a chair.

'Sit down, have you just got off the plane?'

'Why yes,' said Keith, surprised.

Thomas Johnson nodded towards his case. 'Not a detective of your calibre, I'm afraid but the bag was something of a giveaway. Tell me, no doubt you've done well in your chosen career, all the hallmarks of success were there in you as a young man. What rank are you now?'

'Chief Inspector,' Keith admitted.

'Of course you are, of course you are. You are one of those rare cops, good at your job but still compassionate. You've kept your compassion, have you, Keith, you still care about people?'

'I hope so,' said Keith.

'So that is why it's you of all people who have come to tell me you have found Janey's body. You'd have let no one else do it, I know that and I appreciate it.' Keith opened his mouth to speak. 'Before you start, let me fix you a Scotch, I think we both need one.'

Keith wasn't in a position to argue, he certainly needed something. The two men were silent as Thomas poured two generous whiskies into impressive cut glass tumblers. There was no suggestion of water or ice.

'A single malt,' he said, handing it to Keith. 'I may have lived in America for most of my adult life but I have never gone down the Bourbon road, and all that ice, Jesus! Cheers Keith, thanks for coming.'

'Cheers,' said Keith. He took a hasty gulp, it

was very fine indeed. He placed his glass deliberately on the table beside him and looked up at the old man sitting, waiting expectantly opposite him. 'You're right, of course,' he said, 'we have found Janey's body, but this is going to come as something of a shock and there is no way I can prepare you for it. It was the body of a forty-six-year-old woman, she didn't die at seven years old, Mr Johnson, she lived, she married, she bore children.'

There was an electric silence in the room and then, to Keith's horror, the man before him started to weep.

'Give me a moment,' he said and stumbling to his feet, he disappeared down a passageway leading off the sitting room.

Keith sat in silence and then, glancing at his whisky, downed it in one. When Thomas Johnson returned a few minutes later he appeared completely composed. 'But you say she is dead, she is dead nonetheless?'

Keith nodded. 'It is not a good story, Mr Johnson, I don't know if you would like anyone to be with you while I tell it to you, or whether you'd like to absorb first what I've told you so far? I'll do this any way you like but it is all going to come as an enormous shock, however it is told.'

'The only person I'd like to be with me is you, Keith. You were there at the beginning; you're the only comfort I need. Now stop messing about and shoot. What happened?'

'I'm based in Cornwall now,' said Keith.

'Yes, I remember you were a Cornish boy, you found the big city hard to take I remember.' Keith nodded. 'Kept getting lost,' Thomas smiled, 'as I recall.'

'That too,' Keith admitted.

'Go on.'

'Three weeks ago, there was a crime committed which was almost identical to the one committed against your family. I became involved because the Metropolitan police were getting nowhere and they asked me to help as I was involved in your case. Moira and Ian McAllister had two children, Fiona seven and Edward – Ed, who was only two. Ian McAllister was up in Manchester at a conference, Moira and Ed were killed, stabbed in a very similar way to your wife and daughter and Fiona has gone missing, just as Janey went missing.'

'But that is impossible,' said Thomas, 'whoever, whatever monster slaughtered my family couldn't come back forty years later – forty years later, Keith! – and do the same thing again.'

'That is what everyone thought,' said Keith, 'they made exhaustive comparisons between your family and the McAllisters. There was absolutely nothing to link the two families except that the children all attended the same school and you all lived in the same part of London ... and then we hit on the idea of DNA,' Keith continued. 'There was, of course, no DNA profiling available when the crime against your family was committed but we kept,' he hesitated, 'we kept the clothes, both Katie's and your wife's and we were able to lift blood samples from both of them and make comparisons with the McAllisters. It was then that we discovered that Moira's DNA was identical, absolutely identical, to that of your daughter Katie, so identical that they could only be twins. Moira is Janey, there can be no doubt.'

Thomas Johnson got up and walked over to the window of his apartment. He shuffled slightly, his movements rocky, he had aged a great deal, Keith thought, but then that was hardly surprising. The vigorous young executive who had flown over from Washington bore little resemblance to the shuffling figure before him, but he was still recognisable, the spark was still there.

'All these years,' said Thomas, 'I've believed she was dead but instead, although she met a terrible death, the same death as her sister, she did at least live a life, half a life anyway.'

'Exactly,' said Keith. He too felt restless and stood up and came to join Thomas by the window.

'And the marriage was a happy one?'

'Ian McAllister, her husband, was absolutely devastated by her loss. Her children were great, everyone says they were a model family.'

'And yet the same thing happened to her as happened to her sister?' Thomas turned to Keith; he was very pale.

'Come and sit down,' Keith said, 'please. Would you like the other half of that Scotch?'

'Only if you join me,' Thomas said. Keith replenished the glasses. 'Explain it to me again,' said Thomas, 'it's a lot to take in. Janey, Moira you call her, and her son?'

'Yes.'

'Were found dead?'

'Yes.'

'They were both stabbed?'

'Yes,' said Keith.

'And there is absolutely no trace of the little girl?'

'None,' said Keith.

'What's going on?' Thomas asked, shaking his head and sipping at his whisky.

'There is another thing.'

'Another thing?' said Thomas, 'Dear God, Keith, how much more have you got to tell me?'

'It's something I imagine you already know.'

Thomas set down his glass and looked hard at

Keith, his hooded eyes boring into Keith.

'Ah,' he said, after a moment, 'the DNA. I wondered how far your tests had gone.'

'Yes,' said Keith, 'your wife Caroline wasn't the biological mother of the girls, was she?'

'No,' said Thomas, shaking his head.

'And were you their father?'

'No,' said Thomas, 'but I was their uncle.'

'Are you up to explaining? Please, say if you're not, I can come back.'

'No, no, let's do this,' said Thomas. 'I had a sister, her name was Bridget, younger than me, a lot younger than me, nearly twelve years. Because of that and because she was born late in my parents' lives, she was spoilt and she was a brat from day one, she was always in trouble, right from the beginning, right from nursery school. By thirteen she was smoking pot, all sorts, and by sixteen she was a heroin addict and also pregnant.' Keith said nothing. 'The girls were born premature and both addicted to heroin, we nearly lost them over and over but they made it. My sister wanted nothing to do with them. We came home, me and Caroline, to help my mother care for them and it was during that period, ironically, that Caroline was told she could never have children so we simply took them on and raised them as our own.'

'But what about Social Services?' Keith began.

'They monitored the babies to start with but once it was clear they were being well looked after, they lost interest. My sister and I naturally shared the same surname so the children already had my name. We simply raised them as our own, they *were* our own.'

'But what about your sister?' Keith began.

'She died of a heroin overdose eleven months after the babies were born, she was a no-hoper I'm afraid.'

'Even so,' said Keith, 'you didn't think it was right to tell the girls of their origins?'

'Absolutely not,' said Thomas. 'Who wants to know that their mother was a sixteen-year-old heroin addict who didn't want them, when they could have a mother like Caroline who adored them and would do anything in the world for them?'

'Did they have any side effects from the premature birth and the heroin addiction?' Keith asked.

'Strangely enough,' said Thomas, 'I was going to ask you the same question. At the time of the murders they were fine, a little small for their age, but otherwise fine, doing well at school, no problems. I was going to ask you about Janey, Moira, had she done good?'

'Yes,' said Keith, 'she went to university, read

history and achieved a 2:1. She then became involved with a fledgling company dealing in health products, the company prospered and so did she. At the time of her death she was only working part-time because the children were still small but she had done very well indeed.'

'Good,' said Thomas, 'that's good to hear.'

'The girl's father,' Keith said after a moment. 'Stop me if I'm pestering you too much, but do you know who he was?'

'No,' said Thomas, his voice hardening. 'And to tell you the truth I don't think Bridget did either. It went with the territory – drugs, drink, sleeping around. I don't think she had a clue. She had no permanent boyfriend at the time, that's for sure.'

'But could their start in life in some way be linked with this terrible double tragedy? Why didn't you tell us at the time about the girls' origins?'

'There didn't seem any point, I couldn't see in any way that it was relevant. They were my girls, I wanted to mourn them as my girls. If I had told you their origins, it would have been all over the press, it would have been a double tragedy. Caroline was their mother, she died being their mother, I didn't want that altered. If it had been relevant of course I would have told you, but it wasn't.'

'Are you sure about that?' Keith said.

'Absolutely sure. If there had been any

suggestion of a young man then Caroline and I would have had to involve him before we took over the girls but there wasn't. As I say, Bridget didn't know who the father was, so how could the father?'

'But someone,' said Keith, 'someone has to have a serious grudge against your family.'

'Do they,' said Thomas, 'or was it some weirdo, some random weirdo? After all they let Janey live and whatever kind of childhood she's had, it can't have been too bad or she would not have done so well in her adult life. Do we know anything about her childhood?'

'No,' said Keith, 'it is an absolute blank, we found friends at university but before university there is nothing.'

'And this name, Moira?' Thomas asked.

'Again, another blank, she has all the current paperwork necessary to live her life – passport, national insurance number, all that sort of thing, a marriage certificate of course to Ian, but no birth certificate, no record of a birth certificate. She simply materialised out of thin air, or so it would seem.'

'Dear God,' said Thomas. There was a long silence then he galvanised himself into action. 'You must be exhausted, don't even think about what time it is in England.'

'I'm fine actually,' said Keith, 'I'm probably

high on adrenalin. You can imagine I've gone over and over this in my mind the whole way over the Atlantic, trying to think of a good way of telling you, but there isn't one, is there?'

'You did well,' said Thomas, 'now let's make a plan. There is a guest apartment in the building – have you booked a hotel yet?' Keith shook his head. 'Right, well, stay there then, you'll like it. It's a nice place.'

'Thank you,' said Keith.

'So this is what we'll do. We'll go and have some lunch now and after lunch you can have a siesta and then let's meet again this evening for dinner and talk some more.'

Keith smiled.

'What are you smiling at?' Thomas asked.

'Your management skills haven't left you, Mr Johnson. I'm the policeman, I'm supposed to be in charge but I'm more than happy to go along with the plan.'

Thomas Johnson smiled back. 'Well,' he said, 'there is always a good side to everything. We're going to have to spend some time together talking about appalling crimes, but at least we like each other, right?'

'Right,' said Keith, 'that's certainly true.'

They had lunch in a Mexican restaurant; it was

noisy, the food hot but good, the service speedy.

'I chose this place,' Thomas almost shouted above the din, 'because it's loud, you need to sleep, I need to think, we can't do any more talking now.'

Keith was not about to argue. Having broken the terrible news to a man he both liked and respected, he felt the tension ebbing away from him and suddenly he felt unbelievably tired. When he reached the guest apartment he looked at his watch, it was too late to ring Felicity. Setting his alarm for two hours hence he crawled into bed.

11

It was lovely seeing Ellie and Josh again. In all her obsessing over Keith Penrose, Felicity had forgotten how fond she was of them. They arrived by train and having settled Ellie into the spare room and Josh into the Anchorage bed and breakfast nearby, they booked dinner at Ocean Grill overlooking the harbour.

'We came to a decision on the way down,' Josh said, looking fondly at his daughter, 'we're going to spoil you. You've done so much to help us and we never do anything much to help you so, while we're down, which admittedly is only for two days, you are not going to cook anything more complicated than a cup of coffee. We're going to take you out for every single meal.'

'You can't possibly,' said Felicity, 'it'll cost a fortune.'

'Don't be silly,' said Josh, 'we can both afford it, can't we Ellie?'

'We can,' said Ellie, 'and it's not up for

discussion, this is what we've decided.'

'God, you two are becoming a force to be reckoned with,' said Felicity, fondly.

Josh ordered champagne and, as was tradition, once it was poured, he raised his glass. 'To Gilla, God bless her.'

'Gilla,' said Ellie and Felicity. They drank in silence.

'This is where I always say,' said Josh, 'that nobody could turn an ordinary occasion into a party like Gilla.'

'And I always say the world is a poorer place without her,' said Felicity.

'And I say, "I miss you Mum,"' said Ellie, quietly.

They clinked glasses and smiled at one another. The pain was there still but it was bearable now.

The following morning Ellie borrowed Felicity's car and drove over to Hayle to see Mel, Martin and the children. It was agreed she would have lunch with them which left Josh and Felicity alone. There had been talk of a mammoth walk to Zennor along the cliff path with the idea that Ellie could pick them up later, but it was a miserable day, windy and wet, and so they contented themselves with a walk around the town to satisfy Harvey and then at

Josh's insistence went for lunch at Porthgwidden Beach Café.

'I'll be the size of a whale by the time you two go home,' Felicity protested.

'Rubbish,' said Josh, eyeing her up and down with the raise of an eyebrow, 'very trim you are, Mrs Paradise, very trim and there is a certain glow about you. What's up?'

'Nothing,' said Felicity, studying her menu earnestly.

'Oh, come on, Fizzy, how long have we known each other?'

'Thirty-something years,' said Felicity, grudgingly, 'I'd rather not think about it, Josh, if that is alright with you.'

'I'm going to order a bottle of wine and then you're going to tell all.' Minutes later he poured white wine into her glass and handed it to her. 'OK, armed with Dutch courage, I need to know what is going on. I rather suspect it must be that policeman, Penrose, am I right?'

'How did you know?' Felicity said, astonished, completely forgetting to be discreet in her surprise.

'Well, all around the horrid business with poor old Simon, he was helpful well beyond the call of duty and Gilla hinted to me that something was going on.'

'I did confide in Gilla,' Felicity admitted, 'it

was during my last trip to Oxford, the last time I saw her in fact.'

'He's married, isn't he?' Josh said.

Felicity nodded. 'His wife has emigrated to Australia and he doesn't want to leave Cornwall. It's all a bit of a mess to be honest, Josh.'

'Where is he now?'

'Washington.'

'Good Lord, what is he doing there?'

'Oh, a case he is trying to solve.'

'I see,' said Josh. 'So I imagine Gilla's advice was to go for it?'

Felicity relaxed a little and smiled. 'Yes, of course it was, Josh.'

'Is that what you're going to do?'

'I'm going to stand back and wait for him to make his decision,' said Felicity, firmly.

'Not fight for him?' Josh asked.

'He has a wife and two grown-up children who he loves very much. He is also by nature a very moral man, Josh, not like you, you old rogue. I couldn't possibly apply any pressure, it wouldn't be right.'

'I suppose not,' said Josh, 'it's just you're too young to live alone, Fizzy, and it's been a long time now since old Charlie died. It's time you settled down with someone new.'

'That's rich coming from you, Josh, who has

never settled down in his life!'

'Well, I'm me, aren't I, different from you. Anyway I don't need emotional entanglements with women now because I have my daughter.'

'You're happy together, you and Ellie, aren't you?'

'Deliriously,' he said, 'I can't believe it. I've always liked women, as you know.'

Felicity laughed. 'It has been pretty obvious.'

'No, I don't mean like that, I mean my best friends have always been women, I prefer their company to men. I'm certainly not a man's man,' Josh protested.

'That's another truism if ever there was one,' said Felicity.

'To have a daughter is the most wonderful bonus, I love taking her out, showing her off, listening to her confidences, it is absolutely marvellous and of course I came to fatherhood at just the right age.'

'Whose age, yours or hers?'

'Hers of course, darling, I would have been terrible at all that nappy business and school runs, but a grown-up young woman for a daughter, fabulous.'

'You're an awful man, Josh,' said Felicity, laughing, 'but you have cheered me up.'

'Good, well here is my advice for what it's

worth, and I think I'm speaking for Gilla too – don't let this business with Penrose drag on. Either he loves you enough to stay in England and make a life together or he doesn't. It's a big decision and, as you say, it's not your decision, it's his, but for everyone's sake he needs to get on with it.'

12

Keith woke with a thick head wondering where on earth he was and suffering from jet lag, too much whisky and too much emotion. However a shower put him right and, as agreed, at eight o'clock US time, he presented himself at Thomas Johnson's apartment. Thomas looked even older and more tired than he had a few hours before but his manner was as bright and welcoming as ever, and he ushered Keith into the apartment with real warmth.

'I thought we'd have supper here so we can talk,' he said. 'I've got my housekeeper to prepare a little cold salmon and some cheese and I have a nice bottle of Chablis.'

'This is extremely good of you,' said Keith.

'You've travelled all the way from London to see me, the least I can do is to offer you a little hospitality.' They settled into easy chairs, each with a glass of Chablis. 'I've been thinking, well, you can imagine I've been thinking of nothing else since we spoke earlier, I don't mind admitting it came as something of a shock what you had to tell me.'

'I'm sorry,' said Keith, 'I thought about telephoning you first, but I decided it was probably better to deal with it face to face.'

'No, you were right,' said Thomas. 'The thing is,' his brow furrowed in concentration, 'I don't know what conclusions you've come to, Keith, but it seems to me that the horrors that have happened are because of *my* family, not this new family the McAllisters. It began with us and it remains with us because Moira McAllister was Janey, so whatever happened, whatever maniac out there thinks it is fun to go around murdering women and children, the whole horrible business is all about the Johnsons. Is that the conclusion you've come to?'

'I have to admit,' said Keith, after a moment, 'that my major thoughts on hearing the news of the DNA results were twofold and perhaps not very professional. The first was that after all these years, at least we now know Janey lived to be forty-six and not seven; and secondly, as Janey lived to be forty-six, then maybe Fiona McAllister is still alive.'

Thomas smiled at him. 'That's your problem really, isn't it, Chief Inspector, you're a human being first and a policeman second. Maybe your emphasis is a little misplaced.'

Keith smiled in return. 'Possibly,' he admitted.

'I remember you so well,' said Thomas, 'it was

you who picked me up from the airport, do you remember?'

'Yes, of course,' said Keith, 'I will never forget it.'

'I knew of course what had happened, I'd been told by some poor cop here in Washington who had been given the job of breaking it to me and then I had spoken by phone to Scotland Yard, to your boss Chris Lewisham. However, it was you who filled me in on the details and did it with great care and kindness for such a young man.'

'I hope I got it right,' Keith said.

Thomas didn't seem to hear him. 'And it was you who took me to the mortuary to see Caroline and Katie, and you who took me back to my family home, and now here you are again. I am very grateful.'

'It was a terrible, terrible thing that happened to your family,' said Keith. 'If we did anything to ease some of the suffering, then good.'

'I imagine it must also have affected you a great deal, I remember you telling me it was Katie's death you couldn't bear.'

'That's true,' said Keith, 'it was quite strange really, we were clocking off for the day, the boss and I, and then this call came through on the radio – a standard domestic, it sounded like. A neighbour had heard some shouting and screaming and a general kerfuffle going on. Normally in those circumstances, unless there was a complaint from the actual people involved, we would have just sent a constable around to check that everyone was alright, but instead, as we were passing close by, Chris Lewisham made the decision to pop in and see all was well.'

'I bet there have been many times when you have regretted that decision?' Thomas said.

'Yes and no,' Keith said. He stood up and walked over to the window staring out at the apartment block opposite, trying to present his thoughts in a way that was both truthful and yet not hurtful. He turned to face Thomas. 'Your daughters have haunted me all my working life. Katie's death, and the fact that we were unable to help Janey, have provided a yardstick against which I have judged many things, many people, and they have left me with a horror of crimes against children. I have spent most of my working life in Cornwall and compared with many inner cities, the level of violence, man's inhumanity to man, is relatively low. I lost some children in a house fire a few years ago, I lost a Romanian girl, little more than a child, in a fatal stabbing but on the whole there are few crimes against children down in Cornwall. We have a fair number of lost children, visitors mostly, but they are always found again.

The case finished Chris Lewisham, you know, he couldn't bear not being able to solve it, he took early retirement.'

'I didn't know,' said Thomas, 'I'm sorry about that.'

'It's we who should be sorry,' said Keith, 'we didn't find the murderer and we didn't find your daughter.'

'Do you suppose the same man can be responsible for both crimes?'

'You're supposing it is a man,' said Keith.

'Well, wouldn't it be? Women rarely kill children.'

'That's true,' said Keith, 'the exception is, and it's a brutal truth, if women do kill children, it's usually their own.'

'Really,' said Thomas, 'how does that work?'

'Children who die at the hands of their parents are either the victims of violence in the form of drunkenness, drugs or uncontrolled anger, or they are used as a weapon against a spouse; women kill their children to punish their husbands and husbands kill their children to punish their wives.'

'God, what a world,' said Thomas.

'It is thankfully rare,' said Keith, 'and I agree, on the whole, women don't kill children.'

They helped themselves to the salmon and salad from a side table.

'So,' said Thomas, 'where do we go from here?'

'Well,' said Keith, 'assuming that you are right and the problem stems from your family, are there any skeletons that we should know about?'

Thomas sighed. 'The obvious one on my side of the family is my sister Bridget, but we've discussed that.'

'Would there still be any friends of Bridget's who you can remember, who we could contact and who might be able to shed light on who she spent time with during that period?'

'You mean the father of the children?'

'Yes, I suppose I do.'

'I don't think so,' said Thomas. 'She had some friends at school but I can't remember their names now, they would be in their sixties of course. Once she started to get involved in drugs, to be honest, we never knew who her friends were.'

'Caroline then, what about her?'

'Caroline's parents were very traditional, her mother never worked, her father was a bank manager. By the time Caroline and I got together, her parents were both dead and so was my father. My mother, of course, was alive and it was she who initially took the girls on when they were released from hospital following their birth. Caroline has a sister, or had a sister but we've lost touch I'm afraid, she is quite a difficult woman, very critical.'

'What is her name?' Keith said, reaching into his pocket for his notepad.

'Her name is Deirdre. Deirdre Edwards. She is married, or was married to a chap called Harry and they had one child, a boy called Jason.'

'So how old would all these people be?' Keith asked.

'Deirdre was three years older than Caroline, so that would make her nearly eighty now, I've no idea how old Harry was but I imagine two or three years older than Deirdre and the boy, let me think, he must have been in his early teens when the murders happened, fifteen or something like that which would make him mid-fifties now.'

'And you haven't kept in touch, isn't that slightly strange?'

'Not really,' said Thomas, 'I'm over here, they are over there, they moved a short time after the murders and went up to Scotland, I don't know whereabouts. They made no effort at all to keep in touch with me and to be honest I wasn't particularly fond of them so I let the thing lapse. Keith, I've had to find a way of going on living since what happened to my family. I know Caroline and I were separated and it was permanent. We were going to get divorced, but there was no real animosity between us, we just fell out of love and wanted to lead different sorts of lives. I tried to persuade her to come to Washington with me, but she wouldn't.'

'Would the children's true parentage have come to light when you applied for American visas?'

'I don't think so, I think we would have got around that one alright. She genuinely didn't want to come to Washington and nor did she want to spend the rest of her life with me. I'm very, or I was very work-orientated, work always came first, ahead of everything.'

'I think my wife would sympathise with Caroline,' said Keith.

'But you've managed to hold on to her?' Thomas said.

'I'm not sure,' said Keith, 'probably not.'

'Do you want to talk about it?'

'No thanks,' said Keith.

'Fair enough.'

Over coffee plans were made. 'I will need a DNA sample if that's alright,' said Keith. 'I've got the kit with me, it's in my room.'

'Fine,' said Thomas, 'with what purpose in mind?'

'To establish what you say, that you are related to the girls even though your wife wasn't. It just leads credence to your story, I hope you understand.'

'Of course,' said Thomas.

'The team back in England are trying to find out more background on Moira – like when she stopped being Janey and became Moira. They are checking records at university, parental information that sort of thing. I've asked them to e-mail me what they find so I'm hoping that by the time we meet again tomorrow morning I'll have some more answers. It is very hard to imagine how a little girl traumatised by the death of her mother and her twin could be raised by someone else without coming to the notice of the authorities. There was a nationwide search for her, after all, and a mass of publicity.' He smiled at Thomas. 'I seem to be haunted by twins.'

'Really?' said Thomas.

'I had a case a few years back, grown-up twins this time, adopted and raised by different families. Very different men: one a decent chap, one not so decent, one died and one lived.'

'Don't tell me,' said Thomas, 'it was the good guy who died, right?'

'I'm afraid so,' said Keith.

'That's usually the way of it,' Thomas said sagely.

By the time Keith left Thomas Johnson's apartment, he was exhausted but also aware that it was early morning in St Ives and that he could ring Felicity. She answered the phone immediately.

'How are you, where are you?'

'I'm knackered,' said Keith, 'but OK. I'm in Washington at the moment.'

'How's it going?'

'Alright,' said Keith, 'we've covered some ground. I'm not sure we've made much progress but …'

'Can you tell me about it?' Felicity asked.

'Not really, not at this stage.'

'OK.'

'Did you have a nice weekend with Ellie and Josh?'

'I did.'

'You sound a bit odd,' Keith said.

'It's just, well I shouldn't be troubling you with this.'

'What?' Keith asked.

'I think I'm being followed again.'

'Are you sure?' Keith asked.

'I think so and Harvey thinks so too. It stopped while Josh and Ellie were here and to be honest I forgot all about it, but last night when I took Harvey for his usual walk, I'm sure there was somebody watching the house and I'm sure they followed me.'

'Well, for heaven's sake keep your door

locked.'

'I will try,' said Felicity, 'it just doesn't come naturally.'

'Just do it, please, and if you feel threatened in any way ring Jack Curnow. I'll be speaking to him later, I'll warn him you might be in touch.'

'Don't worry Keith, I'm fine.'

'Well, take care and be safe, I'll be back as soon as I can.'

Keith turned off his mobile and put his head in his hands – everything was getting too much. He knew that if Felicity felt she was being stalked, the chances were that she was, she was rarely wrong. But by whom and why and in St Ives of all places? He was missing her and he was worried and he still had made no contact with Barbara and while he felt this trip to see Thomas Johnson had been justified on all sorts of levels, he did not really feel he was getting very far. Except perhaps for Caroline Johnson's sister, there was nothing new and surely to God, Graham Sinclair would have been on to that one already, although there had been no mention of it in any of the files he had pored through. He tried to cast his mind back to the original case; had they interviewed Deirdre Edwards? He couldn't remember her. Maybe Chris Lewisham had done it. Certainly even if she had been in the loop at the time, it was likely she would have been dismissed as being unconnected with the murder. He glanced at his watch, it was too early to ring Jack Curnow really but with a young baby he was bound to be awake.

'Good morning, sir,' Jack said in response to the call.

'More like good night, I think,' said Keith.

'What time is it?' Jack asked.

'I don't know, one-ish, something like that, at night.'

'Past your bedtime then sir,' said Jack.

'You sound very pleased with yourself for this time in the morning,' Keith said.

'I think I've had a breakthrough with the farm thefts and therefore on the death of May Farrell.'

'Really, what sort of breakthrough?' Keith asked. 'I could do with some good news.'

'Well, you know the cattle lorry was abandoned just off the A30 near Bodmin?'

'Yes,' said Keith.

'It belonged to a farmer called Steve Pascoe.' Keith was about to interrupt but decided to let Jack talk. 'Mr Pascoe reported the lorry as having been stolen and so we assumed that he was in the clear.'

Keith let out a sigh of relief. 'So, he's not a suspect then?'

'He is now,' Jack said. 'Mr Pascoe can't give us a satisfactory alibi for the evening May Farrell died, his wife has left him and the farm appears to be on the verge of bankruptcy. The bailiffs have called several times to take things away.'

'And you think because he's in financial trouble, he has started stealing things from other farmers?' Keith said in a challenging voice.

'Well, yes, I rather think I do,' said Jack.

'Steve Pascoe is a good man,' said Keith, roughly.

'You know him, sir?'

'I've known him all my life,' said Keith, 'we were at school together and our fathers farmed not far from one another, both families were friends. Steve has never put a foot wrong as far as I'm aware.'

'Have you seen him recently, sir?' Jack asked.

'No, no,' said Keith, 'not for some time, some years I suppose, now you ask.'

'I think you might find he has changed a lot,' said Jack, 'neighbours say he has not been the same since his wife left.'

'I can't believe Margaret left him.'

'I think it was the drink and the bills just got too much for her,' said Jack. 'Anyway he's a regular drunk now, he's been in some fights and then the whole money thing is out of control, people get desperate.'

'Steve would never wantonly kill somebody.'

'Well, it wasn't intended, was it? He was

driving too fast and he ran her down, it doesn't mean he meant to do it – it happened because he was stealing cattle at the time. I was going to wait until you got back, sir, and then suggest we got him in for questioning, but in the circumstances ...'

'I certainly can't do it,' said Keith, 'you'd better get him in and arrange for someone else to question him with you.'

'I'm sorry to be the bearer of bad tidings,' said Jack. 'Are you making any progress in Washington?'

'A bit,' said Keith. 'I'll ring off now ... Oh, Jack, Felicity Paradise thinks she might be being stalked.'

'Good lord,' said Jack, 'why?'

'I have absolutely no idea, but you know what she's like, she is usually right.'

'That's true,' Jack said, 'do you want me to go and see her?'

'Well, only if you've got the time. I told her to call you if she was worried, I'll be back in the next thirty-six to forty-eight hours, it can probably wait until then but I just thought I'd let you know that she might be in touch.'

'Fair enough, sir, I'll look after her if she's got any problems and, sir.'

'Yes,' said Keith.

'I'm sorry about Steve Pascoe. I really had no idea he was a mate of yours.'

'That's OK,' said Keith, 'you weren't to know.'

13

Pascoe and Penrose – their teachers called them the 'two peas in a pod'. They looked alike – strong wiry boys with masses of unruly hair – they were mad about rugby, they liked riding fat ponies flat out across Bodmin Moor, they surfed, they dived off dangerous cliffs into treacherous seas, they camped in the woods – in short they had a marvellous boys' childhood, free in a way it would be impossible now, Keith thought sadly. They had been friends from when they could first walk to the teenage years and then they had drifted apart. Steve Pascoe, a good-looking boy, had been very popular with the girls; he enjoyed a drink and fancied himself as quite a man about town. Keith, on the other hand, was shy and studious and certainly no big drinker. Then Keith went off to London and they did not see one another for years, except occasionally at mutual friends' weddings. Keith tried to remember when he had last seen Steve – it had to be fifteen years ago. They had bumped into one another in Lemon

Street, Truro, and gone for a quick pint on Lemon Quay. It had been awkward, they had nothing really to talk about, nothing in common any more, and in the end they had got through the half hour they had spent together by reminiscing about their childhood. Was Steve capable of stealing from other farmers? While Jack was right that the killing of May Farrell had been an accident, the concept of Steve not stopping having hit the poor woman ... He had always been the wild one, he led and Keith followed but even so ...

Keith undressed and climbed into bed. Lying there in the dark, his mind whirling, he was unable to sleep although he was dead tired. It occurred to him that outside his family and work colleagues he had made very few friends over the years, real friends, anyway. Being a policeman separated you in so many ways from normal socialising, people were always a little wary of you. He must remember to tell Jack that, to hold on to his good friends. He could do with a good friend right now, Keith thought, to help him see the wood from the trees, to help him decide what to do for the best.

When he woke the following morning there was an e-mail from Graham Sinclair which was far from encouraging. On Moira's university application form she had quoted both her parents as being dead and her next of kin as a London-based firm of solicitors. Graham had contacted the solicitors who mercifully were still practising. The partner who had dealt with Moira had died some years ago, but his son was now senior partner and remembered the case. He had been doing his articles at the time but his father had talked to him about the client. A sum of fifty thousand pounds had been deposited in the client account by the trustees of Moira's dead parents. He remembered that another set of solicitors had been involved and he rather had the impression that they were based abroad but he could not remember where. No records remained and once again the trail had gone cold.

Keith checked out of the apartment and called on Thomas Johnson for the last time.

'Fifty thousand pounds,' Thomas said when he heard Keith's news, 'that's a tidy sum now but it was a monstrous amount of money back then.'

'And you really have absolutely no idea who could have funded that?'

'No,' said Thomas, 'I don't.'

'Did the girls have god-parents?'

'No, they weren't christened; our view was that we should leave it up to them to decide their own faith when they grew up. Deirdre is the only person left alive – assuming she is still alive – from the time of the murders who has any close relationship to us and the girls.'

Embarrassed, Keith took a DNA swab from Thomas' mouth and promised to be in touch when the results came through. Then the two men shook hands.

'I don't expect I will ever see you again, Keith,' said Thomas. 'You have played such a pivotal role in my life, but I never visit England and I don't expect you come to Washington too often?'

'First time,' said Keith, 'not that I've seen anything of it.'

'Shame you can't stay and I could show you the sights.'

'Not a chance I'm afraid,' said Keith, 'but thanks for your hospitality.'

'It was a pleasure,' said Thomas, 'and I really mean that. Safe journey.'

Keith finally arrived back in Truro at eight forty-five the following evening. He was too tired to go anywhere but back to the family home. Even the bleakness of it failed to upset him – he was too exhausted to care. From the train he had rung Felicity and explained that he needed to stay in Truro overnight; what he didn't tell her was it was not just about tiredness. Jack had called to tell him that Steve Pascoe had not only been taken in for questioning but had broken down, confessed and been charged with theft and manslaughter. The thought sickened Keith and he resolved to go and see Steve first thing in the morning. He just couldn't believe it, there had to be some sort of mistake.

When he awoke the following morning in the bed he had shared with Barbara for so many years, his sense of disorientation seemed to magnify. Determined not to dwell on it, he showered, dressed quickly and headed into town. Jack met him at the police station.

'You're really sure Steve Pascoe is responsible?' Keith asked.

Jack looked crestfallen. 'I am and I am so sorry he is a friend of yours, but there is no doubt – the man has confessed and he knows all the details of the various thefts. I am sure he was a nice chap once, but he is a mess now, sir, he really is.'

And so he was. If Keith had not known who he was, he would have had difficulty recognising him. He had put on an enormous amount of weight, yet around his face his features were haggard, his eyes bleary, red-rimmed.

Before Keith could even speak, Steve shouted across the room. 'I thought you would turn up like a bad penny sooner or later, come to gloat, have you? Well, gloat your fill, Keith.'

'I'm not here to gloat, Steve,' said Keith,

drawing out a chair and sitting across the table from his old friend. 'Is there anything I can do to help?'

'Bit late for that now, isn't it? I could have done with some friends back along when Margaret left me, but it's too late now for anyone to help me, especially you.'

'I'm sorry,' said Keith, 'I hadn't realised things had got so bad for you.'

''Course you hadn't, too busy being important Chief Inspector Keith Penrose just flown in from Washington DC. I should feel honoured, I suppose, that you've even taken the time to come and see me.'

'Oh, for heaven's sake, Steve, don't be ridiculous. You've confessed to some very serious crimes, are you really guilty?'

''Course I am.'

'Are you sure? This is serious stuff, a good woman died, Steve. I just can't believe it, that you just left her to die.'

'Just shut the fuck up,' said Steve, 'I don't have to listen to this, and I don't want to see your ugly mug ever again, always so high and mighty, always better than me at everything, well, you've certainly proved your point now, haven't you?'

Keith stood up and stared down at the man before him. 'It's not my fault the way you are, Steve, it's no one's fault but your own. You must have seen that woman in the path of your lorry and having hit her, anybody with an ounce of compassion would have stopped. You're not someone I even know any more, you disgust me.' Without a backward glance, he strode out of the room, shutting the door none too quietly behind him.

Jack, who had been watching the interview from the viewing platform, met Keith outside the door. 'I did warn you, sir.'

Keith nodded and hurried off down the corridor, without a word.

'Could I suggest, sir, you go and have some rest? You look awful,' Jack called after him.

Keith stopped and turned around. 'I'm fine. You haven't heard anything from Mrs Paradise, I take it?'

'No,' said Jack, 'I was going to call her but we've been so busy here. Would you like me to do so?'

'No, no,' said Keith, 'I'll get in touch with her.'

Keith returned to his office and spent the next hour on the phone being debriefed by Graham Sinclair as to his various conversations with Thomas Johnson.

'You sound as if you like him,' Graham said at the end of the interview, 'and trust him. You believe he is telling the truth, I take it?'

'As far as I know,' said Keith. 'It was hard, I haven't seen the man for forty years. We've both changed a lot in that time but he seemed genuinely anxious to help, that's all I can say, I suppose, but where that leaves us I'm not sure. Are you going to interview the sister?'

'You mean Caroline Johnson's sister?' Graham asked.

'Yes, Deirdre.'

'Well, here's a thing,' said Graham, 'she lives on Mull.'

'Oh no,' said Keith, 'I've just got back from Washington.'

'I'm only joking,' said Graham. 'You never met her, did you?'

'No,' said Keith, 'I presume someone must have interviewed her but it wasn't me.'

'Washington was different, you had a relationship with Thomas Johnson. One of the DIs is going up to see her tomorrow. We were wondering if you would come up to the Yard again on Monday and spend a day in the incident room, we'll have the information back from Mull by then.'

'Just remind me,' said Keith, 'what day of the week is it today?'

'Thursday,' said Graham, with a laugh, 'so you've got a few days to pull yourself together.'

'Great, thanks,' said Keith. 'I'll see you Monday, I'll catch the early train and I should be with you by ten-thirty.'

'That'll be fine.'

14

'Oh my lord,' said Felicity, coming down the stairs at Jericho Cottage to meet Keith. 'Just look at you.'

'What's wrong with me?' Keith asked, smiling and taking her in his arms.

'Just about everything I would say, you look exhausted. What first – a bath, a sleep, a drink, a meal?'

'I can't go to bed until bedtime,' said Keith, 'or else I'll never get myself straight again. I think a drink and a talk is what I need.'

'Come on up then, I've lit the fire in the sitting room. I'll fix you a drink and you can collapse on the sofa, how does that sound?'

'Brilliant,' said Keith, 'as long as you will collapse with me.'

'Consider it done.'

Settled with a glass of red wine in front of the fire, Keith looked apologetically at Felicity as she sat down beside him and took his hand in hers. 'I can't tell you much about the Johnson/McAllister case, it's all hush-hush at the moment.'

'Damn,' said Felicity, 'I was dying to know why you went shooting off to Washington in such a rush, and now you're saying you are not allowed to talk about it.'

'I'm not, I'm afraid,' said Keith, smiling. 'If the press got hold of the information we now have, it could be dangerous for Fiona.'

'I'm not going to talk to the press, am I?'

'I know, but there are rules,' Keith began; he looked away, embarrassed suddenly.

'What is it?' said Felicity.

'It's different.'

'What's different?'

'Well, Barbara was never interested in my work. She saw it as the enemy, she would rarely want to talk about any of my cases.'

'Which in a way I guess must have made it easier,' said Felicity.

'In a way you're right, but please, please don't stop taking an interest, just not this one and at this moment.'

Felicity held up her hand. 'You don't have to explain any more, that's fine.'

'There is one thing I would like to talk about.'

'What?' Felicity asked.

Keith took a sip of wine and put down his

glass. 'Can I have a hug?'

'You certainly can. What's wrong, there is something wrong?'

'You know those farm thefts and the poor woman who died at Towednack?'

'Yes.'

'The guy responsible was my best chum when I was a kid.'

Felicity drew away and stared at him. 'You have to be joking, you poor, poor man. When did you find out?'

'Jack did all the donkeywork, it was nothing to do with me. Steve, my friend, was taken into custody when I was on my way back from Washington but by the time I arrived in Cornwall he had been charged – he confessed in fact.'

'Would you ever have thought he was capable of such a thing?'

'No,' said Keith, 'not at all.'

'Come here, no more talking, you must have done enough talking in the last few days to last you a lifetime.'

Over breakfast the next morning Felicity studied a considerably more relaxed and rested man and decided to take the plunge.

'Keith, have you talked to Barbara yet and told her about your job?'

'No,' he said, studying his coffee cup.

'I thought you might have found the time with all that hanging about for trains and planes.'

'It wasn't really appropriate and there was precious little privacy anywhere.'

'Has she not been in touch with you?'

Keith shook his head.

'It's a bit odd, isn't it?'

'Maybe, I don't know,' said Keith, 'we've never been great communicators, Barbara and I. I guess that's one of the problems.'

Felicity took a deep breath. 'Only I'm finding this situation quite difficult.'

The man, who had been starting to relax, visibly tensed before her eyes. She felt awful.

'I know, I know,' he said, running a hand through his hair, 'but I just can't do everything all at once. This Johnson case, you being stalked, my best childhood chum up for manslaughter, losing my career so suddenly. I can't. I just can't ...' his voice trailed away.

Felicity put a hand on his arm. 'Stop my love, I understand all of it, you don't have to explain to me the pressure you're under. I just think it might be better if we had a little break from one another.'

'What?' said Keith, staring at her incredulously. 'You can't mean that?'

'I do.'

'But the weekend is coming up.'

'Exactly,' said Felicity. 'What you need to do is to go back to your home and do a lot of sleeping, relaxing and thinking and at some point over the weekend, touch base with your family. I'm not suggesting you make the big decision this weekend, I'm just suggesting you find out how they all are and at the same time tell them about your redundancy. I think you're putting off talking to them at all because you feel you've got to decide what you're doing finally, but you don't need to decide right now. They must think it's really odd you haven't been in touch.'

'They could have rung me.'

'Could they, with the hours you keep? Where were you the day before last, Washington, for Heaven's sake?'

'I thought this weekend we would spend together,' he said, forlornly.

'So did I,' said Felicity, 'until I started thinking things through. You're winding yourself up tighter and tighter and ...' she hesitated.

'And what?' Keith asked.

She stood up, went over to the Aga and took the kettle off the hob. Then she turned to face him. 'I love you coming home to me, I love us being together, but the more I am with you, the more I want to be with you.'

'So why …' Keith began.

'Listen,' said Felicity, 'I don't know yet whether you're going to go back to Australia, I don't know yet whether you're going to make a life with your family out there. The pull must be very strong, you're a good man and you want to do the right thing. My problem is the more I see you the more I want to see you, the more I'm with you the more I want to be with you.' She looked down at the table, blinking back tears. 'Forever,' she whispered.

Keith stood up and scooped her into his arms. 'God, I am a selfish bastard,' he murmured into her hair.

'No,' said Felicity, against his chest, 'you're just a man with a problem, a big one.'

'I can't live in Australia so the decision is made really.'

Felicity drew away from him. 'There you are again, just take one small step at a time. Ring the family and tell them about your redundancy. They didn't make a big fuss about you coming back to the UK because they knew you had to come back for your job. Now you haven't got a job for much longer, you don't know what sort of pressure they are going to apply and how you are going to react to it. It may be that they have taken on board that really you would rather live in Cornwall, regardless of whether you are working or not, or they may assume that the sole reason you are back here is because of your work. If you really can't live in Australia then you need to tell them that, and having told them, then Barbara has a straight choice, you or Australia.'

'She's made that choice already,' said Keith, 'she's made it quite clear and I have to say I can understand. She has lived her life around me and my work and now it's her turn.' He hesitated. 'It's odd, I've spent so many years coping with the fall-out from other people's awful emotional problems and I've never really had one of my own. Yes, there was the dreadful worry about Carly when she was diagnosed with Hodgkin's, but that apart, aside from the usual domestic dramas, my personal life has just drifted by. Every now and again, Barbara would blow up about my work and my lack of involvement with the children and we'd have an uncomfortable few days and then things would go back to normal.'

Felicity regarded him with interest. 'So you took no notice of her?'

'It's not that I took no notice, I didn't think there was anything I could do about it.' He glanced at his watch. 'Heavens, I'm going to be very late to work, I should have gone ages ago. Should I call you tonight?'

'If you want to,' said Felicity, 'it's up to you,

there's no pressure at all from me, just take your time and decide what you want to do.'

'I know what I want to do,' Keith said.

Felicity regarded him sadly. 'Come on, I'll walk you down to the front door.'

They were both in the hallway. 'Will you take care,' he said, 'any more feelings about a stalker and you'll let me know?'

Felicity nodded. 'Now off with you,' she said, with a smile.

He picked up his briefcase and headed out of the door. She watched him as he walked up the road to Barnoon car park and only when he was out of sight did she allow herself to cry.

15

'We're bringing Jason Edwards in for questioning,' Graham Sinclair phoned to inform Keith later the same morning. 'You can have a talk to him when you come up on Monday if you want.'

'All the way from Mull,' said Keith, 'did you need an extradition order?'

'Very funny,' said Graham, 'we probably will in a year or two's time.'

'What makes you think this is worthwhile? You must be pretty sure of your facts to drag him all the way down to London.'

'He's an oddball, he's never married, there is something a little different about him, Asperger's or something like that, and he has been done for sexual harassment – twice.'

'I don't see what that has got to do with anything,' said Keith, 'these murders have been brutal executions. There is no hint of sexuality involved in either of them.'

'Nonetheless, the sexual harassment charges

spell of instability.'

'It spells to me a lonely middle-aged man with problems who can only get near a woman by making unwelcome advances; it doesn't make him a murderer.'

'Our DI thought there was a case to answer. He was sixteen at the time of the Johnson murder which puts him at nearly fifty-seven now, so he is quite capable of having committed both crimes and he knew the victims.'

'He didn't know the McAllisters,' Keith objected.

'He didn't know the McAllisters, but he did know the Johnsons very well, they were his first cousins and Moira McAllister was of course as we now know, Janey Johnson.'

'You are surely not suggesting that Jason Edwards knew all along that Janey hadn't died?'

'We don't know what we're suggesting yet, but Jason is the only person close to the families who is capable of having committed both murders.'

'And that's grounds for bringing someone in?' said Keith. 'If I presented a mythical murder to a bus queue of twenty people, I bet I would find at least eighteen out of the twenty would be physically capable of murdering them in the right circumstances.'

'You're just being awkward now, Keith,' said

Graham. 'Anyway, let's not argue about it, he's coming down to London today and you will be able to talk to him on Monday if you so wish. I think it could be helpful since you were so involved in the original case. Have a good weekend.'

By the time Keith had replaced the receiver he was in a fine old temper and he was missing Felicity acutely. He had a whole weekend to get through and clearly the Met were arresting the wrong man, if arresting was what they were going to do. Then to cap it all Jack put his head around the door. 'Your mate Steve wants to see you again,' he said.

'Well, I don't want to see him,' said Keith.

'He says it is important.'

'Incidentally, who got the confession out of him?' Keith asked.

'Neil Mavers,' said Jack, making a face.

'That pillock, he probably bored Steve to death so he confessed just for a bit of peace and quiet.'

'Come on sir, you know that's not right, Steve did it all right.'

'I suppose so,' said Keith. 'Alright, I'll go and see him.'

Steve looked better. He had shaved and had been given clean clothes; he stood up as Keith came into the room and held out a hand. Keith took it wordlessly.

'I'm sorry, boy,' Steve Pascoe said, 'I had no right to say those things to you. This is my mess, I got myself into it and I have nobody else to blame, certainly not you. It was just the final straw seeing you. God I wish we could turn the clock back and start over.'

Keith sat down and Steve followed.

'So,' said Keith, 'is there anything I can do for you, a lawyer, anything?'

'No, that's all fixed up, thanks,' said Steve.

'I'd be happy to stand as a character witness if you'd like me to.'

'No,' said Steve, 'no, I really wouldn't. I don't want to damage your position in any way. Besides, you can't really give one, the boy I was is nothing like the man I became. I could tell when you came in here the other day you barely recognised me and that is just the outside – inside I'm different too. My troubles have been of my own making but that doesn't make them any easier to bear. I'm sorry about that old lady though, I truly am.'

'Then for heaven's sake tell the judge and jury that, over and over,' said Keith. 'You can't say it enough.' There was a silence between the two men. 'My sergeant said you wanted to see me.'

'Only to say sorry,' said Steve, 'and to wish you well.'

Keith stood up. 'I wish you well too, Steve.'

'In a strange way,' Steve said, also standing, 'it's almost a relief, everything is out in the open now, no secrets. I'll lose the farm, go bankrupt but at the end of the day, does it really matter? I let a lot of people down and killed a nice old lady, I deserve to be punished.'

This time the two men embraced wordlessly and Keith walked out without looking back. His mind was full of the boy Steven Pascoe had once been, full of fun, mischief, laughter, not a care in the world – what a waste.

Felicity had to keep busy. She spring-cleaned the kitchen, took down all the curtains in the cottage and put them through the washing machine, then she scrubbed out the hall and the top step and finally returned to her bedroom to look at it with a new and critical eye. It was a bit girly, she had to admit. If Keith was going to be a permanent part of her life she would probably need to do something about it, the important word being 'if'. It would be humiliating to do anything dramatic now and then find that he didn't come back. She sat down on the bed. Of course he would come back, and yet everything Felicity knew about Barbara indicated that she was a strong woman – and if Barbara decided that Keith was to live in Australia with her and the children, there was a good chance she would succeed. The bedroom had better stay as it was.

The front door bell rang, making her jump. She got up and shouted at a barking Harvey to be quiet. She opened the door. Annie stood on the newly-scrubbed step.

'I'm here because I think I was a bit harsh with you the other day, my girl, and now I see you're spring-cleaning the place, that's a sure sign you're troubled. Your inspector is back in town, I see.'

'How did you ...?' Felicity stopped in mid-sentence, there was absolutely no point in asking. 'I don't want to talk about him, Annie, but I'm sure you were right to be angry with me.'

'No I wasn't, girl. If that wife of his was stupid enough to go off to live in Australia when it is not what he wants to do, then she has only herself to blame if he doesn't follow her.'

'I honestly can't talk about it,' said Felicity, 'I'm just ...' Her words trailed away miserably.

'Alright then, but you can come down to the Sloop and buy me a glass of port,' said Annie.

'I'm filthy, an absolute wreck,' said Felicity.

'Sloop won't mind, come on girl, do you good.'

While Felicity was drinking in the Sloop with Annie and a group of friends, Keith had a hot bath followed by a solitary supper in front of some mindless television. Tomorrow he would ring Barbara but tonight he decided to think of as little as possible and keep his mind as blank as he could. He decided that since he wasn't seeing Felicity, he would go up to London and stay there until some progress was made on the Johnson/McAllister case. That being the case he would take on the challenge of the Sunday train service and travel up during the day so that he would be bright and early on Monday.

At the same moment as Keith turned out his bedside light, Felicity said good night to her friends in the Sloop and with Harvey sauntered back towards Jericho Cottage. It was only as she turned into the lane by the cottage that she again had the strong sense of being watched; someone was lurking in the shadows behind her. Harvey too pricked up his ears. For a moment she was tempted to turn around to face whoever it was, but her courage failed her.

'Come on Harvey,' she said and together they hurried up the lane and through the purple door, Felicity locking and bolting it firmly behind her.

It is amazing what a person can find to do in order to prevaricate and avoid the job in hand. Keith unpacked his bag and repacked it for London. The house was immaculate so there was nothing he could find to do there. Anxious to keep busy, so he went out into the garden. He brushed down the paths and did a little weeding. Then he came back inside, made a cup of coffee and cleared the fridge of anything he thought would not be edible by the time he returned from London. He looked at his watch. It was still only nine-thirty, but there was no way he could avoid it any longer. He found the piece of paper in his diary and punched in Barbara's number. She answered almost immediately.

'Good heavens, Keith, where are you ringing from?'

'From home,' he said.

'From the landline?'

'Yes.'

'I'll call you back in a few minutes, I have a special number that makes it almost free.'

'Oh, OK,' said Keith; he replaced the receiver and stared at it accusingly. Having psyched himself up he didn't want this sort of delay. It was nearly ten minutes before Barbara rang him back.

'Sorry for the delay,' she said, 'but it is worth it. How are you?'

'Fine,' said Keith, 'and you?'

'Absolutely fine, it is starting to get quite autumnal here but it is still so lovely and warm and the sun never stops shining, it is marvellous, Keith.'

'I'm sure it is,' said Keith. 'How are the kids?'

'Both blooming, Will has a new girlfriend, an Australian girl, lovely, all blonde and brown and leggy, you know how they are. He is besotted and it seems pretty mutual.'

'Good, good,' said Keith, 'and Carly?'

'Carly is fine. Everybody is working very hard except me, although I have a part-time job now.'

'Really?' said Keith.

'Yes, I'm teaching in a local primary school, just two days a week.'

'Teaching what?' Keith asked, intrigued.

'A little history, a little English, a little geography – I'm a bit of a fill-in really, but I'm enjoying it.'

'I'm sorry I haven't been in touch,' said Keith.

'It's OK, I know why you haven't.'

For a moment Keith's heart flipped a beat. 'How do you mean?' he asked, cautiously.

'I've been Skyping your sister and she told me all about the Johnson case and the new murders. Awful. Are you getting anywhere?'

'Not really,' said Keith, 'we have a few leads. Barbara, there is something I have to tell you.'

'Go on,' said Barbara.

'I'm being given early retirement, compulsory not voluntary.'

'Are you, Keith – why?'

'Thirty-year rule,' said Keith, 'anyone who has served in the police force for thirty years or more is being laid off.'

'Were you expecting it?'

'No, not really,' said Keith, 'the whole thing blew up while I was in Australia.'

'When do you finish?'

'In June, end of June, I've got three months.'

'How do you feel about it? No, don't answer that,' said Barbara, 'Having been made redundant myself, I know how you feel about it, it's your life. Are you still not wanting to come out here?'

'Not really,' Keith managed.

'There will be some pressure from the children once they hear you are stopping work.'

'And from you?' Keith said, cautiously.

'No, no pressure from me, I've told you that all along. I've decided what I'm going to do with my life, you must do the same. Anyway, I'd better ring off now, I'm meeting some friends for a drink.'

'OK,' said Keith, 'well, send my love to the children, I'll ring them soon.'

'Will do, goodbye Keith.'

Keith replaced the receiver and stared around the kitchen at what had once been his home and now was just a house. Barbara had been neither cold nor unkind. It was almost worse, she was just not terribly interested. He didn't know what he had expected, but somehow after all the years they had lived together, he had expected more of a reaction. It was ironic really, he was filled with guilt about his feelings for Felicity but his wife seemed simply to have moved on without a backward glance or any sense of guilt. Maybe it was a cue to do the same.

16

Keith walked into Graham Sinclair's office at the Met at nine o'clock sharp on Monday morning expecting a welcome. Instead he was met with considerable hostility.

'Have you seen these?' Graham challenged.

Keith looked at the newspapers spread out before him. 'No,' he replied, 'I haven't seen the papers, I've come straight from the hotel.'

'Just look at the headlines,' Graham said.

Keith walked round to Graham's side of the desk and his heart skipped a beat. "Janey found after forty years ... dead. Moira is the missing girl who died like her sister forty years on. Police couldn't solve it last time, will they do any better now? Nephew held for questioning." The headlines ran on and on.

'Whoever leaked this?' Keith said.

'I thought perhaps you had,' said Graham.

Keith stared at him, genuinely bewildered. 'I thought we agreed that we were keeping the press in the dark about this.'

'We did agree it,' said Graham, 'but someone has leaked the story, and it isn't me.'

'And it certainly isn't me,' said Keith.

'Maybe you discussed the case with somebody down in Cornwall?'

'I discussed the case with no one. Oh, I suppose there is one possible exception.'

'Who's that?' said Graham, still accusing.

'Well, I did discuss it with Thomas Johnson, but I think we both agree there would have been little point in spending the tax payers' money on a trip to Washington unless I told him the full story. It's possible he leaked it to the press, I suppose to put pressure on us to perform.'

'I hardly think so,' said Graham.

'Neither do I,' said Keith, 'and I also can't imagine why you think it is me who would have leaked the story?'

'Because you're not happy with the way we're running the case,' said Graham.

'I admit I wasn't happy about your reluctance to run DNA tests and I'm not happy about the nephew,' said Keith. 'I haven't met him, but it seems to me grossly unfair to put a vulnerable man through the trauma of interrogation when his profile just doesn't fit. I also deeply resent the suggestion that I would go to the press to vent my spleen. If I am not happy with the way an investigation is going I tell my colleagues – not the press.'

'Well, try this,' said Graham, clearly unrepentant, 'Jason was staying with the Johnsons up to twenty-four hours before the murders.'

'Why?' Keith asked.

'You may well ask.'

'I *am* asking,' said Keith. 'It was October, surely the boy should have been at school?'

'Exactly,' said Graham, triumphantly, 'he wasn't at school because he had been expelled.'

'And are you going to tell me why he was expelled?' said Keith.

'Yes, I am,' said Graham, 'he was expelled for being violent. Violent to another boy, the boy ended up in hospital, nothing serious and no bones broken but badly bashed about.'

'And what reason did Jason give for the attack?'

'He wouldn't discuss it,' said Graham, 'but talking to his mother I gather he was being bullied. Sounds like the bullying was the other way around though, doesn't it?'

'Not necessarily,' said Keith. 'If we are talking about somebody who is vulnerable, he probably *was* bullied at school and finally, in desperation, lashed out.'

'He is autistic,' Graham admitted, 'but only mildly so. I don't really think that is justification for putting a fellow pupil into hospital. It also shows that he can be violent and he has got a temper. I just don't understand why you are so against the possibility of Jason being our man, particularly as you haven't even met him.'

'I'm not against it,' said Keith, 'I just don't think it is very likely.'

'Or could it be,' said Graham, 'that you are reluctant to consider him because you and Chris Lewisham missed him the first time around?'

Keith sat down heavily in the chair opposite Graham. 'Oh, for God's sake, Graham, I am three months off retirement, I don't give a fig about my reputation, or Chris Lewisham's come to that, because nothing can hurt him now. All I want is to solve a case which has haunted me my entire working life. If you honestly think that I am the sort of man who would be anxious to cover his tracks, then you really don't understand me at all, and I am probably wasting my time here.'

At last, Graham Sinclair had the grace to look abashed. 'I'm sorry,' he said, 'you're right, I had no call to make such an accusation about a cover-up or the press leak, come to that. I'm just very confused as to why you are utterly rejecting this line of enquiry.'

'We're missing something, something absolutely fundamental,' said Keith, 'something that has been staring us in the face and we just can't see it – and Jason Edwards isn't it.'

'Do you want to talk to Jason?'

'Yes, I would like to,' said Keith.

'You won't get much out of him, he is pretty monosyllabic.'

'He is probably frightened,' said Keith.

Graham raised his eyes to heaven.

'Before I see him,' said Keith, 'do you have the transcript of Chris Lewisham's interview with Deirdre? I'm assuming he interviewed her, I know I didn't.'

'Yes,' said Graham, 'there is nothing much there but she neglected to mention that her son had been staying in the house until shortly before the murders, which, in itself is significant.'

'And what does she say about that now?'

'She says she can't remember whether she mentioned it or not and, of course, with Chris no longer with us, there is nothing we can do to verify that statement.'

'Where was she at the time of the murders?'

'She was at home, she alleges with Jason, at their home in Richmond. The first she heard about it was a frantic call from Thomas who was in Washington. Then, of course, she was interviewed by Lewisham and considered to be irrelevant to the line of the enquiry.'

'And Jason wasn't interviewed at all?'

'No, it would appear not. We asked him the question when he was first arrived here and he said he couldn't remember.'

'Not an unreasonable reply,' Keith suggested.

'I think you would remember as a sixteen-year old boy if you had been interviewed by the police following the murder of your aunt. It is not the sort of thing you are likely to forget, is it?'

'Maybe not,' Keith conceded, 'people do blank things though, don't they, particularly things they don't want to remember? Tell me, what does Jason do?'

'He works in a fish-packing factory,' said Graham, 'not exactly mind-stretching for an ex-public school boy.'

'So you are trying to fit him up for the Johnson murders, but what about the McAllisters, has he an alibi?' Keith asked.

'Only his mother again.'

'So you are suggesting that he left Mull, travelled down to London, murdered the McAllisters and got back again and nobody missed him?'

'It just so happens,' said Graham, triumphantly, 'that he was on a week's holiday, so no one missed him at work because he wasn't supposed to be there.'

'So you reckon he booked his week's holiday so he could come down and murder the McAllisters,' Keith said, trying, but failing, to keep the sarcasm out of his voice. 'And incidentally what has he done with Fiona?'

'Look, Keith, I don't know what is bugging you but there is nothing more I can say. Just go and see the man and see what you think for yourself.'

'I'll certainly do that,' said Keith.

Jason Edwards looked exactly as Keith had imagined, in fact it was almost uncanny the resemblance the man had to Keith's image of him. He sat hunched at the interview table, an untouched cup of tea before him, his head was bowed, his shoulders drooping. Keith knew him to be fifty-six, yet in a strange way he seemed younger, he was very overweight so there were few lines on his face and there appeared a childlike quality about him even before he opened his mouth. Keith moved quickly across the room and sat down opposite the man, anxious not to intimidate by standing over him.

'You've not touched your tea,' he said.

'I don't like tea,' said Jason.

'Coffee?'

'Or coffee.'

'What do you like?' Keith asked.

'Water,' Jason replied, 'but not out of a tap, out of a bottle and it has to be cold.'

Keith looked up at the young police sergeant in attendance. 'Arrange it, would you please?' The sergeant hesitated. 'Just do it,' Keith said.

'Do you know why you're here?' Keith asked Jason gently.

Jason nodded miserably. 'They think I murdered people, my aunt, I didn't, I would never hurt anyone.' The whole time he was speaking Jason continued to stare at a spot somewhere on the floor to the right of him, eye contact seemed beyond him.

'I am sorry we dragged you all the way down from Mull, but it is really important we find out who murdered these poor people. Whoever did it could murder again.'

'Yes,' said Jason, still staring at the floor.

The sergeant appeared at the door with a bottle of water and handed it to Keith.

'Here is your water, Jason,' said Keith, 'would you like a glass?'

'No,' said Jason, 'I drink it straight from the bottle.' He pushed his tea away and opened the bottle of water, drinking from it greedily.

'You were thirsty,' Keith said.

'I've been asking for water ever since I arrived, but they would only give me water out of a tap. I can't drink that.'

'I'm sorry,' said Keith. 'Do you remember staying with your aunt before she was murdered, you were just a boy, sixteen?'

'Yes,' said Jason, 'yes, I remember.'

'Did you like your aunt?'

'I did. She, she …' he paused, 'she was more fun than my mother.'

'In what way fun?' Keith asked.

'She made me laugh and she wasn't always telling me what to do …' he hesitated, 'I felt …'

'Go on,' said Keith.

'I felt grown up, the same as her, she didn't treat me like a kid.'

Keith looked thoughtfully at his bowed head. 'I have to ask you this, Jason, and I apologise in advance, but did you have a sexual relationship with your aunt?'

For the first time Jason's eyes left the floor and flickered briefly up at Keith.

'No,' he said, 'no, of course not. I've never had a sexual relationship with anyone.'

'I didn't mean to upset you,' said Keith, 'but I'm a policeman, I have to ask these questions, do you understand?'

'No,' said Jason, 'I don't understand and I don't

know why I'm here.'

'OK,' said Keith, 'keep calm Jason, we've nearly done with this. Tell me why she made you feel grown up.'

'Because she told me stuff.'

'Told you what stuff?'

There was a long pause before Jason replied. 'Told me about her marriage, that it was over, that she was going to get a divorce.'

Keith frowned.

'That's all,' said Jason, 'she didn't want to live in America, she didn't want the girls to be raised in America but her husband would not give up his job and live in England.'

'Was she sad about it?' Keith asked.

Jason considered the question for some time; he took so long that Keith nearly repeated his question, but was glad he didn't.

'Yes,' said Jason, 'I think she was sad, but she was angry, too. She felt her husband, his name was Thomas, was being selfish.'

'Did you kill her, Jason?' Keith asked.

'No,' said Jason, 'of course not.' Once more his eyes flickered to Keith's face briefly. 'I wouldn't be able to kill anyone and why would I kill her? I liked her, she was really kind to me.'

'Is there anything which happened during that last holiday you had with your aunt which was odd, different? It doesn't matter how small a detail, something, anything that might help us?'

'I don't know what you mean,' said Jason.

'Did you go anywhere, see people?'

'The girls were at school during the day. While they were at school I usually did some gardening and sometimes my aunt took me out to lunch. Then when we collected the girls we would just go home for tea and homework.' His face brightened, 'We went to the zoo, London Zoo, one weekend and another time we went to the Science Museum, I liked that.'

'Did friends come to the house much?' Keith asked.

'No, not much, the girls had friends. Sometimes a friend would be dropped off with them or sometimes one or both of them would go to a friend's house.'

'Did Caroline have any friends, a boyfriend perhaps?'

'Oh no,' said Jason quickly, 'no boyfriend, she was still married you see, but she did have some women friends, mostly the mothers of friends of the girls. She saw them sometimes, not very often though, she didn't go out much except with me and the girls, she was frightened to, I think.'

'Frightened?' said Keith, trying to keep calm, trying to keep the excitement out of his voice, he had to be so careful. 'Why was she frightened, Jason?'

'She thought someone was watching the house.'

'And how long had she thought that?'

Jason shrugged.

'How long did you stay with her?' Keith asked, carefully.

'I don't know, a few weeks? I had been expelled from school, Mum was angry with me and Caroline said I could stay with her and help with the girls.'

'So was she afraid all the time you were staying with her?'

'No,' said Jason, 'just towards the end.'

'How near the end, the week before, days?'

Jason frowned, all his concentration still appearing to be aimed at the same spot on the floor. 'I can't remember,' he said.

'Try,' said Keith, 'help me.'

They were the right words.

'I want to help you,' Jason said, 'I don't want the man who killed my aunt to get away.' He continued to frown in concentration. 'I think it was about a week before I left she asked me if I had noticed anything. We looked out of the window and there was a man standing in the shadows on the opposite side of the road, she said he had been doing it before but I had never seen him before.'

'What did you think, were you worried?'

Jason hesitated. 'I think, I thought she was making a fuss about nothing.' He suddenly raised his head and looked straight at Keith. He had very fine eyes, bright blue and piercing. 'But she wasn't making a fuss though, was she?'

'Did you know Caroline Johnson thought she was being watched?' Keith demanded as he strode back into Graham Sinclair's office.

Graham frowned. 'No.'

'That is what Jason Edwards has just told me. It slipped out at the end of the interview. I was asking him about her friends and he told me that she didn't go out much and that she thought a man was watching the house.'

'At the risk of sounding a bit like Mandy Rice Davies,' said Graham, 'he would say that, wouldn't he.'

'Oh, for Christ's sake,' said Keith, 'the man is innocent, you must see that? While we're messing around with him we are losing precious time to find that little girl. Anything could be happening to Fiona. We don't know that because her mother was safe forty years ago that she is too. We don't even know how closely the crimes are connected and you're wasting your time trying to pin the murder on a confused, vulnerable man who clearly is not capable of murder, or anything else much of a physical nature, just because it is convenient.'

'Have you got a better idea?' Graham asked.

'No,' Keith conceded. 'Presumably you've been pulling his house apart while he has been down here. Has Forensics found anything?'

'No,' said Graham, 'neither he nor his mother like the smell of fish so the moment he comes home every night he strips off all his clothes and she puts them straight in the washing machine, very convenient.'

'Oh come off it,' said Keith, 'you really are clutching at straws. You're going to have to release him, he has nothing to be charged with, and you know that.'

'Yes,' Graham admitted, 'we will have to let him go, I can't argue with that, but he is weird and he has no satisfactory alibi for either of the murders.'

Keith chose to ignore him. 'How did he get here?' he asked.

'We had a car pick him up from Oban, he was escorted on the ferry over from Mull.'

'Well, make sure you drive him back again.'

'What!' said Graham. 'We can't afford to do that, or rather the taxpayers can't.'

'There is no way Jason is going to be able to

cope with public transport back to Oban, and frankly why should he? I got more out of him in fifteen minutes than you did in two days of questioning, and why? Because I didn't frighten the living daylights out of him. If you had got some local copper to interview him in his own home, not only would you have saved the taxpayer a lot of money but you'd have found out everything you needed to know. It is so typical of the Met, assuming provincial coppers can't do their job properly. You brought him down here, you make damn sure you take him back.' Keith rose to his feet.

'Anything else?' Graham said, raising an eyebrow.

'No,' said Keith.

'Where are you going?'

'I'm off to pursue some enquiries of my own,' said Keith.

'You'll need to keep me informed.'

'I'll keep you informed if I have anything to report,' said Keith and he strode out of the office without a backward glance.

17

The little girl awoke to find herself in an enormous armchair, so big it seemed it must belong to a giant. She ran her arm over its red leather which was soft and leaned back comfortably in the squishy cushions which surrounded her. She seemed to be very high off the ground, her feet nowhere near touching the floor. She was feeling quite comfortable, sleepy but comfortable and then suddenly panic struck her with such a force that she gasped. Where was she? Terrified, her gaze darted around the room and settled on a man sitting in the twin chair to her own, they were separated by a brightly burning log fire and a colourful rug over a wooden floor. The man looked very old.

'Hello,' he said.

'Hello,' said the little girl, 'where is my mummy?'

'Don't worry about your mummy now,' he replied, 'you're fine, you're safe.'

'I want my mummy,' the little girl repeated.

'Listen,' said the man, 'what can you hear?'

The child, momentarily distracted from the strangeness of her surroundings, cocked her head and listened.

'The sea,' she said, 'I can hear the sea.'

'You can,' said the man, smiling, 'and tomorrow we will go and see it, look for shells and watch the waves.'

'Will Mummy be there?'

'Not tomorrow,' the man said.

The child began to cry, quietly. 'I just want Mummy,' she said, 'where am I?'

'Somewhere nice and safe. Look, I want you to meet someone.'

A woman stood in the doorway and just for a fleeting second the child thought it could be her mother, then she saw the woman was much older.

'Hi there,' the woman said.

'This is Miss Reeny,' said the man, 'she is going to look after you. She is really kind, you'll like her.'

The child stared at the woman, her sobs subsiding for a moment; she felt so tired and her head ached, she felt a little sick. Everything was so strange, hardly real at all. The logs crackled in the grate, her eyelids grew heavy and she gave in to sleep. It seemed the safest place to be.

'Jack, how are things?'

Jack Curnow was sitting at his desk wading through paperwork and trying to stay focused. His boss's voice immediately had him on red alert. Something was up, hopefully. 'Hello sir, all is quiet here, in fact nothing is going on at all.'

'Don't sound depressed,' said Keith, jauntily, 'in our line of work nothing to do means success.'

'If you say so, sir,' said Jack.

'The Pascoe case?' Keith asked, cautiously.

'He's being committed for trial so that's what I am doing now, wading through the paperwork and putting all my ducks in a row. Not that much to do though really, seeing he has confessed.'

'When is the trial?' Keith asked.

'About three months, I think, that's the general feeling. He will be kept in custody until then, there has been no bail application.'

'Really,' said Keith, 'but why no bail? On a manslaughter charge with no previous, surely he should get bail?'

'He doesn't want it,' Jack cut in, 'he has nowhere to go, his home is having to be sold, he knows he is going down for a stretch and that remaining in custody now will count in his favour. His thinking is he might as well get on with it, take his medicine and get the whole mess behind him.'

'Makes sense, I suppose,' said Keith.

'I think so,' said Jack, 'he has changed so much

from the angry man who came in. He now recognises what he did was terribly wrong and is wanting to make amends. If it is any comfort sir, I think his current attitude will go down well with the judge, he is deeply remorseful.'

'That's good to hear,' said Keith, gruffly.

'How are things going your end?'

'Badly,' said Keith.

'Strange sir, you don't sound as though it's going badly, you sound positively ...' he hesitated, looking for the word, '... energised.' He was tempted to add more energised than he had been for months, but had the good sense to keep quiet.

'The Met are hopeless, they are making a complete hash of this case,' said Keith, 'so I've decided to go it alone. There is a little girl who needs finding, I don't believe she is dead, but wherever she is, she needs to be returned to her father.'

'I agree, sir,' said Jack, thinking of his own daughter, 'that is the absolute priority.'

'You wouldn't think so the way the Met are going on. Anyway, what I was wondering was whether you would fancy a few days in the Smoke?'

'What, come up to London?'

'Absolutely,' said Keith, 'and help me.'

'I wouldn't mind ...' Jack began.

'I don't know how Maggie will feel?'

'She'll be OK,' said Jack, 'she is absolutely gutted about what is happening to you, the redundancy and all, there is nothing she wouldn't do in the next few months to support you.'

'That's good to hear,' said Keith, 'tell her how much I appreciate that.'

There was a silence between them. 'What about the "Super", what is he going to think? He is not going to like you going out on a limb, is he?'

'Probably not,' said Keith, 'but leave him to me, I'll sort him out. You just get on the first train you can – will you come up today or tomorrow?'

'Could I catch the first train tomorrow morning, sir. It would just give me a chance to sort things out at home.'

'Of course,' said Keith, 'I'll meet you in the morning at Paddington at ten.'

'Sir, it's Keith Penrose.'

'Hello Keith,' said George Staple, 'how's it going?'

'Not especially well,' said Keith, 'I have a favour to ask you.'

'Go on,' said George, immediately relieved. He was still feeling bad about the way he had handled Keith's redundancy, or rather the way he hadn't handled Keith's redundancy – he was anxious to make amends.

'This McAllister case is going nowhere,' said Keith, 'the Met are tramping about in hobnail boots but somehow we're missing the obvious. They arrested a relation of the Johnsons simply because he was the right age to have committed both murders and also has learning difficulties. It's ludicrous and everybody has lost focus. What we should be trying to do is find that little girl. Just because her mother didn't die in the first round of murders, the Met assume that Fiona isn't going to die in this one.'

'I suppose it's not an unreasonable assumption,' said George.

'The cases are linked, of course they are linked,' said Keith, 'but that doesn't mean they are going to be dealt with by the perpetrator in the same way.'

'So,' said George, 'where do you go from there?'

'That's just it sir, I admit I've had a bit of a row with the Met and so I've asked Jack to come up to London and help me for a few days.'

'That could make things a little difficult, politically.'

'Will it sir? Surely no one needs to know especially.'

'Let me get this straight,' said George, 'what you are saying is you want to branch out on your own investigation and you want your trusty sergeant along with you?'

'That's about it, sir.'

'And have the Met given you a brief to do this?'

'Absolutely not,' said Keith.

'I see,' said George.

'Two thoughts,' said Keith, 'one is when you made me redundant you did ask me whether there was anything you could do to help, well this is it, sir. I have spent most of my professional life haunted by this case. If I could crack it I could take the whole redundancy thing on the chin.'

'And the other?' said George.

'How great would it be if Devon and Cornwall beat the Met at their own game.'

'Your first reason has merit,' said George, 'but your second is undeniably irresistible.'

'I thought you might think that, sir,' said Keith.

Felicity Paradise and her dog, Harvey, were standing on top of Clodgy Point in a minor gale. Normally this particular place made Felicity feel better, the magnificence of the cliffs and the rolling seas usually putting everything into perspective, but today she was just downright miserable. She had spent months, years, loving Keith Penrose in one form or another and now, when it seemed there was a real chance of their being together, she had sent him away. Why? For some absurd reason of pride, to test him, to test herself? She had absolutely no idea – all she knew was that without him, life didn't seem worth living.

Two things happened simultaneously; a shaft of sunlight came out from between two angry storm clouds and lit the sea below her, and her mobile phone rang.

'It's me,' said Keith.

'Hello,' said Felicity, tremulously.

'Good God, where are you? You sound like you're in a wind tunnel.'

'I am, sort of,' said Felicity, 'I'm on top of Clodgy.'

'It sound like it's blowing a real hoolie.'

'It is,' said Felicity.

'Then come down from there, for heaven's sake, it's dangerous.'

His proprietorial manner thrilled her but she certainly wasn't going to admit it. 'Don't boss me around, Chief Inspector,' she said, 'me and Harvey are having a walk.'

'It doesn't sound a very responsible walk to me,' said Keith. 'Look, I've got a lot to tell you but I can't compete with that wind, can you give me a ring when you get home?'

'I certainly can,' said Felicity. She replaced the

mobile in her pocket and gazed around her. The sun was turning the tips of the waves golden; last year's bracken glowed; suddenly the world was a very different place.

An hour later Felicity returned Keith's call.

'Where are you?' she asked.

'In London, in an awful hotel,' said Keith.

'You sound …' she hesitated, 'chirpy.'

'I don't know why,' said Keith, 'but I am somehow. Basically, I've told the Met to get knotted and I've got permission from the "Super" for Jack to come up and join me to help crack this case.'

'Goodness,' said Felicity, 'that sounds a bit dramatic – the Penrose Police Force.'

'Something like that,' said Keith, smiling, 'but now the press have the story and it is in the public domain, I can fill you in on the whole thing and three heads are better than two, particularly yours, Mrs Paradise, who has been known to have a nose for these things.'

'I think you are confusing your metaphors,' said Felicity, 'heads and noses and all that.'

'Oh never mind,' said Keith, 'are you sitting comfortably? Then I'll begin.'

When Felicity switched off her mobile half an hour later, her mind was racing. Why had Janey been spared in the first murders only to be killed in the second? Why in both murders had one child been killed and the other left alive? How could one man commit two murders forty years apart?

'Could I come and see the scene of the McAllister murder?' she had asked Keith.

'I'll have to get permission myself,' said Keith, 'but I want to see Ian McAllister in any event, so I will ask him rather than the Met. You're hoping for one of your little moments, I assume?'

'Well, I want to do anything I can to help. There would be no harm in me taking a look, would there, if he doesn't mind, poor man?'

'Certainly not,' said Keith, 'I will be back to you on that one, it might take a day or two.'

She was back involved in his life and the relief was enormous. They had not talked about their future, of Barbara, of whether he should be returning to Australia. He was totally focused on solving this case and she was totally focused on helping him. That was all that mattered for now.

18

Ian McAllister was a nice man, Keith decided almost immediately. He looked terrible – there were bags under his eyes, a couple of days' worth of stubble on his chin, his clothes were rumpled, even the way he stood looked defeated and broken, yet despite all that Keith could sense a warmth. Despite everything he had been through, when he smiled, Keith could see it was where his features felt most comfortable. He was of medium height, about the same as Keith, with a shock of fair hair now turning white. Although Keith had made an appointment, Ian McAllister had been wary and uncommunicative when Keith had first entered his house, but now they were sitting comfortably in his kitchen sharing a pot of coffee. The atmosphere had changed between them, now that the purpose of Keith's visit had become clear.

It had begun badly. 'I have told you people a thousand times where I was and what I was doing leading up to my wife and son's murder. You have witnesses galore, if twenty-odd people in the hotel wasn't enough, you've checked out my petrol receipts, everything.'

'I'm not here to check up on you, Mr McAllister,' Keith had said, 'I know you had nothing to do with your family's murders, I'm just here to help.'

That was all it took, the invitation to coffee was almost immediate.

'I got to know what I suppose we should call your father-in-law quite well,' said Keith, 'both forty-odd years ago when he was over here and subsequently I have been to Washington to see him.'

'So I understand,' said Ian.

'He is of the view that the reason for the murders must lie with his family, rather than yours on a sort of cause and effect basis – in other words your wife and son would not have been killed if her sister and mother hadn't died all those years ago.'

'I still can't believe it,' Ian burst out, 'I still can't believe she didn't tell me about it, didn't tell me who she really was.'

'Perhaps she didn't know?' Keith suggested.

'She was seven, that's old enough to remember something as horrific as the destruction of your family. Whoever brought her up may have brainwashed her into believing she belonged to them, but she must still have had memory of what happened and I just can't understand why she didn't share it with me.'

'Tremendous shock does result in children, indeed not just children – anyone – blanking out complete parts of their life.'

'I suppose so.' Ian sounded far from convinced.

'So what did she tell you?' Keith asked.

'Well, now I look back on it,' Ian said, 'not much. I knew her parents were both dead and she was an only child. I knew she had a legacy from a firm of solicitors which presumably was left to her by her family, although come to think of it, she never actually explained, I just presumed.'

'Did she talk about her childhood at all?'

'No,' said Ian, 'with the benefit of hindsight, I can see that it was odd, but she was so caught up in the present. She adored her job and I believe she adored me and certainly the children. Her life was so fulfilled, she was so happy, we both were, it was what was happening now that mattered. We haven't been married all that long, only eight years, we married late you see, both of us having given up on ever finding the right person and then all this ...' he gestured around the house, '... a wife, a home, two lovely children, it seemed too good to be true, and it was.' Tears began running down his cheeks but he made no attempt to wipe them away.

'I'm very sorry,' said Keith, 'I just can't think of anything worse. It is unimaginable what you must be going through.'

'I just want Fiona,' said Ian, 'I keep imagining what somebody might be doing to her, I'd rather she was dead than being, than being ...' He couldn't put his thoughts into words and Keith didn't blame him.

'Where did they live – Moira and her parents?'

'You'll think I'm hopeless, I just don't know,' said Ian, 'she said they had lived all over, that her father travelled a lot and she and her mother usually went with him.'

'Running away perhaps, never staying in one place long for fear of somebody finding out who she really was.'

'Possibly,' said Ian, 'but I still come back to the fact that she could have told me, we trusted each other completely. I just don't understand. These people who raised her, who clearly weren't her parents, do you think she may have been frightened by them, do you think she might have been threatened that if she disclosed their whereabouts her life would be in danger?'

'Maybe that is why she and your son were killed, because she was threatening to tell the truth of who she really was,' Keith suggested.

'But she could have told me the truth and if

she wanted no one else in the world to ever know, then that's how it would have been.' Ian blew his nose vigorously.

'It hurts you a lot that she didn't confide in you, doesn't it?' Keith said.

'Yes it does,' said Ian, 'nothing is as bad as her death and Ed's death, nothing is as bad as Fiona missing but after that, yes. I guess if we had married when we were both younger I'd have been more curious about her family, but we were both mature independent people, a long way from childhood, and if she didn't want to elaborate on her early years that was fine with me ... but to deliberately withhold her past, I can't believe it.'

'Just think really hard,' said Keith, 'was there ever a place that she mentioned, that she was particularly fond of or had been to often, as a child I am talking about.'

'I don't think so,' said Ian, 'I'm sorry I can't help, but I really don't think she ever mentioned anywhere specific. As I say, we were so into the here and now.'

'Would it be possible for me to see the room where the murders took place?' Keith said.

'Yes, help yourself,' said Ian, 'I won't come with you if you don't mind, it's the first door on the right as you head towards the front door.'

'It's strange,' said Keith, 'but this is awfully like

the house your wife was living in up until the time of her abduction.'

'Really?' Ian asked.

'Yes, the layout is almost identical. Coming in the front door with the sitting room on the left then the stairs straight up and the kitchen behind, that's how the other house was.' Keith rose to his feet. 'Who found this house, you or your wife?'

'Moira did.'

'I wonder if it was her choice subconsciously ...' Keith began, then shook his head, and leaving the poor man to his coffee headed towards the sitting room. The sitting room was also very similar to Moira's childhood home, with the fireplace opposite the door and a bay window to the left. He could still remember the scene of the Johnson murder so clearly in his mind. There was no sign now of what had taken place here, there was a new carpet smell and the smell of fresh paint too. Someone had done their best to put the room back to rights, but Keith suspected Ian McAllister had never been back into it.

There were several pictures dotted around the room of the children, the family group and Moira's and Ian's wedding day. Keith wandered about studying each of them. As Ian had intimated, their life seemed cloudless, the children sweet, the parents doting on them and each other, it was there to see in the catalogue of photographs. Keith stared around the room, his heart heavy – another devastated family and still no answers as to why.

Keith returned to the kitchen to find Ian where he had left him. 'I was wondering whether you would mind if a friend of mine had a look at the room, she has some sort of second sight, sixth sense, whatever you like to call it. You probably think it is rubbish but ...'

'I don't think anything is rubbish that might help us find Fiona,' said Ian, 'you can bring along as many people as you like if it will help find my daughter.'

While Keith Penrose was interviewing Ian McAllister, Jack Curnow was at the firm of solicitors, Donovan and Troon, whose offices were at the far end of Fulham Road. Keith had arranged to meet him at a pub nearby afterwards.

'Thanks for coming to rescue me,' said Jack, when they had ordered a glass of red wine and half a bitter, 'I am definitely outside my comfort zone, I'm feeling very much a Cornish boy today.'

'At least you made it here,' said Keith.

'No skill there, I'm afraid,' said Jack. 'When you said you couldn't meet the train, I panicked and took a taxi.'

'So how did you get on?' said Keith, taking a

sip of his red wine and grimacing.

'Not spectacularly well, I'm afraid sir,' said Jack, 'in fact pretty much a dead end.'

'Go on,' said Keith.

'David Donovan is the son of Alan Donovan, Alan was the original solicitor who dealt with Moira. David now runs the practice pretty much, I don't know what has happened to Troon but he is not in evidence, it seems to be a one man band these days. David remembers the case because his father was very intrigued by it. A huge amount of money arrived out of the blue, many thousands of pounds, David can't remember exactly how much, but a fortune in those days. It was placed in their client account and instructions were given to make Moira a monthly allowance and to meet any other reasonable needs. Alan Donovan was effectively her guardian as well as her solicitor, there weren't any trustees, he simply made decisions as he saw fit. Having said that, apparently his task was not too arduous, Moira was far from a wild child and largely lived within her means without too much prodding from him.'

'What was given as Moira's maiden name?'

'Brown,' said Jack, with a rueful smile.

'Hardly very original. How old was Moira Brown when this money and she arrived in Alan Donovan's life?' Keith asked.

'She had just turned eighteen and had applied to Durham University.'

'Did Alan Donovan ask where she had come from or gain any background information?'

'This is where things get particularly tiresome,' said Jack, 'David cannot remember that sort of detail and there are no records left, sadly it was before the days of computerisation and when the files became obsolete they were simply destroyed after ten years.'

'What happened to the money?' Keith asked.

'As soon as Moira turned twenty-one it was released to her and she had nothing more to do with Donovan and Troon, so their association was only for three years,' said Jack. 'I don't expect for a moment that David Donovan would even have remembered it apart from the fact that it was such a large sum of money. Oh, and he did meet her once.'

'Really?' said Keith.

'She rented a little flat in Chelsea, Chelsea Manor Street, and she seemed so alone in the world that Alan Donovan arranged for his son to help her move in.'

'Does he remember the exact address and do we know how long she lived there?'

Jack shook his head. 'It was nearly thirty years ago, sir.'

'I realise that,' said Keith, testily.

'I'm sorry sir,' said Jack, 'I did my best.'

'No, I'm sorry,' said Keith, 'it's just been a rather fruitless twenty-four hours. I decided to go and visit the school that was quoted on Moira's university application form, St Margaret's in Addison Avenue.'

'And?' Jack asked.

'It doesn't exist, and what's more it never did.'

'You would think the university would have picked that up.'

'Again, we are talking pre-computerisation. I imagine if she had a good set of A level certificates they probably wouldn't have checked the school.'

'And did she have a good set of A level certificates?' Jack asked.

'The university was satisfied with them but the Met could find no trace of her actually sitting the exams. They may have been as fictitious as the school.'

'Someone must have helped her achieve all this.' said Jack, after a moment's pause.

'Yes,' said Keith, 'and someone with a lot of money, enough money to give her a generous allowance, a sizeable sum of capital, a flat in Chelsea and a manufactured past – none of that comes cheap.'

'So who and where?' Jack asked.

'God knows,' said Keith, 'so many dead ends.'
The following morning things were looking slightly brighter. A lengthy conversation with Durham University had established that Moira's old tutor still taught there and a discussion with him revealed that Moira Brown had a very good friend at university called Annabel Lucas. The fact that Edmund Goddard remembered his pupil at all was a miracle in itself, the fact that he also remembered her friend was a seriously lucky break.

Annabel Lucas lived in London too; in fact, Professor Goddard seemed to remember that the two girls had actually shared a flat together both up in Durham and during holidays in London. Jack was dispatched to track down Annabel Lucas while Keith picked Felicity up from Paddington station.

They had not met for nearly a week and on the journey up from Cornwall, Felicity had promised herself she would play it cool where Chief Inspector Penrose was concerned, but at the sight of one another they were in each other's arms in seconds, muttering endearments and smiling with the pleasure of seeing one another again.

Keith glanced at his watch. 'We are not due to see Ian McAllister until half past eleven, we've got time for a coffee if you like?'

'Let's get to Fulham,' said Felicity, 'and find

one there. We don't want to be late for the poor man.'

It was a warm spring day and when they arrived in the Fulham Road they found a little café with tables out on the pavement, they ordered coffee and sat and stared at one another.

'We're no good apart,' said Keith.

Felicity shook her head. 'I know but we're not going to talk about it, not now, not yet. Tell me how you're getting on?'

'Not very well,' said Keith, and filled her in on the happenings of the last twenty-four hours.

'This Annabel Lucas might be helpful.'

'If we can find her,' said Keith, 'the thing is though, if Moira didn't confide in her much-loved husband the secrets of her past, is she likely to have told her girlfriend?'

'Possibly,' said Felicity, 'one is often more "warts and all" with girlfriends; with boyfriends you are more likely to present yourself at your best. If the two girls really did live together in London as well as at university, they must have been very close and of course Moira was a lot younger and her childhood a great deal more recent than when Ian McAllister met her.'

'True,' said Keith. He took her hand and squeezed it, 'thanks for coming.'

'I'm not sure I'll be of the slightest use,' said

Felicity, 'but it's a good excuse to see you.'

'What did you do with Harvey?'

'Mel has got him, the children are delighted, I am going to have an awful job ever getting him back and ...' she hesitated, 'and to be honest I was quite glad to get away.'

'Why?' Keith asked.

'I'm sure I'm still being followed, Keith.'

'Why didn't you mention this before?'

'Sometimes I think I am imagining it and, I can't explain it exactly, it doesn't feel threatening, it just feels like I am being watched.'

'Can you describe the person who is watching you?'

Felicity shook her head. 'I think it is a man, but whoever it is, he is good at his job, he is just a shadow. If it wasn't for Harvey I might not even know he existed.'

'Have you told the police?' Keith asked.

'I just have,' said Felicity, with a smile.

'Maybe if we can get back to St Ives this weekend we can see if it is still going on and do something about it.'

'Finding this little girl is the priority, Keith, don't worry about me and my stalker, or whatever he is. As I say, I don't feel threatened exactly, just uncomfortable.'

'Still,' said Keith, 'it needs checking out. Come

on, we had better go now.'

Ian McAllister answered the door before Keith had barely finished ringing.

'No news, I suppose,' he said.

Keith shook his head.

'You've heard nothing from the Met?'

'Nothing at all.'

Keith introduced Felicity. 'I hope you don't consider this an intrusion,' Felicity said.

'Absolutely not,' said Ian, 'as I said to Inspector Penrose, we're clutching at straws now, anything anybody can do to help ...' His voice trailed away.

If anything, Keith thought, he looked worse than he had twenty-four hours before. The horror of his missing daughter must be consuming him. Keith tried to imagine what it would be like if a seven-year-old Carly had gone missing, and failed, it was beyond comprehension.

'Would you like some coffee?' Ian was asking.

They both shook their heads.

'The room is off here to the left,' Ian said. 'Will you go in together?'

'No,' Keith and Felicity replied in unison.

'I'll go alone,' said Felicity.

'Do you want me to explain where everything happened?' Keith asked.

Felicity shook her head. 'Just leave it to me.'

19

Felicity opened the door and walked into the sitting room, closing it firmly behind her and leaving the two men in the corridor outside. As had been Keith's experience, it was the smell which hit her first – new carpet and fresh paint. She walked over to an armchair by the fireplace and sat down and waited. Ten minutes passed and then, with her eyes closed, she began to feel real terror. There were no images in her mind, simply the feeling of terror and then pain but worse than either, the desperate and hopeless attempt to save her child.

When she finally emerged from the room, twenty minutes after entering it, she came out like a rocket, slamming the door behind her and almost running into the kitchen. She was very white and trembling. Keith jumped up and guided her into a chair.

'Would you like anything?' Keith asked.

'Water please,' she managed.

Ian stared at her in bewilderment. 'What

happened?' he asked.

'Give me a minute, could you? I'm sorry.' She took a gulp of water from the glass Keith had given her and for a moment rested her head in her hands. Her head ached and her pulse was still racing. 'I didn't see anything,' she said at last, addressing Ian, 'just feelings, I was feeling what your wife felt.'

'Oh God,' said Ian.

'But there is something,' said Felicity, 'of which I am almost certain.'

'What?' both men said.

'The little girl, your daughter, Fiona, she wasn't there, she wasn't in the room when the murders took place. Your wife tried so hard to protect your son but couldn't, but he was the only child there.'

'But that's impossible,' Ian burst out, 'we know Moira collected Fiona from school, she talked to several people outside the school gate and she had Ed with her. They drove home and when she was helping the children out of the car, one of our neighbours passed by, an old lady who lives just up the road. She babysits for us occasionally and she might be old but she is totally on the ball, there is no way she would have made a mistake. She was ...' his voice cracked, 'she was the last person to see my family alive. It was about half past four and they were altogether then.'

'Maybe Fiona went around to a friend's house?'

Keith suggested.

'In which case we would know about it, and she would be alive and safe,' said Ian. 'They went into the house and they never came out. Anyway, Mrs Paradise, how do you know Fiona wasn't there?'

'I don't know,' said Felicity, 'but this gift of mine, or curse or whatever you would like to call it, is usually pretty reliable, though not infallible. I just felt what your wife felt and she wasn't concerned about your daughter because your daughter wasn't there, that is all I can tell you.'

'What, what did she feel?' Ian asked, stammering over the question.

Felicity lifted her eyes and gazed at him. 'Do you want me to tell you?'

'I'm not sure. Did she suffer?'

'Yes,' said Felicity, 'but her primary concern was for your son, that is where her agony really lay, she was much less concerned for herself.'

'Of course,' said Ian.

Felicity was struggling. 'Mr McAllister, it didn't last long, that I can promise you. It was over very quickly.'

There was a long silence in the room broken at last by Felicity again.

'There is a good side to this,' she said at last.

'I was thinking that,' said Keith.

'Two things, if Fiona wasn't there to witness

the murder of her mother and her brother, then she will be a lot less traumatised than we had imagined and ...'

'... and,' Keith continued, 'maybe she was taken away before the murders quite deliberately because like her mother before her, the intention was she should survive.'

'But,' burst in Ian, 'if someone went to all this trouble to give Moira some secret childhood we know nothing about, why in God's name, wait until she has two children and a happy life and then kill her and her son?' He burst into racking sobs.

Felicity got up and slipped an arm around his shoulders, pulling him to her like he was a small child. He sobbed against her for a few minutes and then drew away.

'Sorry.'

'Don't be,' said Felicity. 'I'm not sure whether I have been any help or not but I truly believe Fiona was not in that room.'

Felicity still felt very shaken when they finally left Ian McAllister. 'Where are we going now?' she asked as they stepped out onto the pavement.

'I'm going to buy you some lunch,' said Keith.

'I'm not hungry.'

'You will be, something light to help settle you. Come on.' He took her arm. Just then his mobile rang; it was Jack.

'I've found Annabel Lucas,' he said, 'she is Annabel Havers now, she is a yummy mummy who doesn't work. Where are you, sir?'

'Still in Fulham, I have Mrs Paradise with me.'

'My geography is not all that good but her house is in Sydney Street which is in Chelsea somewhere. I've made an appointment for us to see her at two-thirty, is that alright?'

'Perfect,' said Keith, 'give me the address and I'll meet you there at two-thirty.'

'Would you mind if we just went back to Ian McAllister for two seconds?' Keith asked, when he had finished with his mobile.

Felicity shook her head. 'Why?'

'I'll explain to you in a moment.' They walked the few yards back to Ian McAllister's house and pressed the bell. He took a long time to answer this time, and when he did it was clear he had been crying again. 'Sorry,' said Keith, 'do you know a Annabel Havers?'

Ian shook his head.

'She used to be a friend of your wife's, she was Annabel Lucas then, they were at university together and their tutor believes that they shared a flat in London too.'

'My wife had a flat in Chelsea Manor Street,' Ian said.

'That's the one,' said Keith, 'and this Annabel Havers now lives in Sydney Street.'

'That's just across the King's Road only a few doors away.'

'Really,' said Keith, 'sorry being a Cornish lad, I am not great at finding my way around.'

Ian managed a ghost of a smile.

'It's odd,' said Keith, 'Moira and Annabel seemed to have been inseparable at university and yet you've never met her. She wasn't at your wedding?'

'We had a very quiet wedding, we married at Chelsea registry office with just a couple of witnesses from work. Neither of us wanted a big do,' said Ian.

'It is odd though, isn't it?' said Keith.

'I suppose so,' said Ian.

'Anyway, we are seeing her this afternoon so if I've got anything useful to tell you, I'll give you a call.'

'Thanks,' said Ian, dully and closed the door.

'That man is in so much pain,' said Felicity, as they walked away down the road.

'Are you surprised?' Keith said.

'No, no, of course not but I'm certain he is no way responsible for what happened.'

'Me too,' said Keith. 'Look there is a little Italian across the road there, let's give it a try.' He took her arm and shepherded her across the road. Not surprisingly neither of them had much appetite; they ordered some bread and olives, a salad and a glass of red wine. There was so much to talk about, and inevitably they talked of Keith's meeting with Annabel Havers.

'If anybody can throw light on Moira's past, it's going to be her, isn't it?' said Felicity. 'This could be the breakthrough you need.'

'Let's hope so,' said Keith.

'It's odd though,' Felicity said.

'What's odd?'

'Well, with all the publicity surrounding this case you would have thought she would have come forward of her own volition and not waited to be found.'

'Unless,' said Keith, 'she feels she has nothing to tell us.'

'Maybe,' said Felicity.

Keith hesitated. 'I know it can't have been a good experience but can we talk about what you felt and saw in that room where the killings happened?'

Felicity took a sip of her wine. 'I saw nothing, I felt the mother's pain, her terror, her concern for her little boy but the girl, Fiona, definitely wasn't there, I am absolutely certain about that as much as I ever can be with my weird feelings.'

'They are not usually wrong,' said Keith.

'No,' Felicity admitted, 'but if she wasn't in the room, Keith, then where was she?'

Keith shook his head. 'I don't know, but as we said if she has been kidnapped and survived, then the fact that she didn't see her mother and little brother die, it means she has a much better chance of a near normal life to live with her father if we could just find her.'

'Do you think she is alive?' Felicity asked.

'Yes I do,' said Keith, 'but more importantly, what do *you* think?'

'I have no true feelings about it,' said Felicity, 'just the obvious conclusion that if it is a copycat of the Johnson case then there is a good chance that she *is* alive.'

'Oh God, if only I could make sense of it all.' Keith looked anguished.

Felicity put out her hand and took Keith's across the table. 'You have to be heading in the right direction.' She squeezed his hand and smiled at him. 'It is the only logical way forward. If you can find out what happened to Moira during her childhood then that is where Fiona will be, it has to make sense.'

'You'd think so, wouldn't you?' said Keith. 'Well maybe Annabel Havers can help us. What are you going to do this afternoon?'

'Go home,' said Felicity.

'Do you have to?' Keith asked, looking totally crestfallen.

'I think I do,' said Felicity, 'I'm going to be in the way if I stay here.'

'You're not,' Keith said.

'I am. You and Jack need to do some serious thinking but if you do get a day off over the weekend come back to St Ives.'

'I didn't think I was allowed to do that,' Keith said, 'I thought we were putting some distance between us.'

'As you said,' Felicity answered, gently, 'we're not much good apart. Come home Keith, we've got a great deal to decide and talk about but while this little girl is missing we shouldn't be wasting any energy on that. It was wrong of me to add to your pressure, I was just feeling, well, insecure I suppose, which is ridiculous at my age.'

'Of course it isn't,' said Keith, 'we love one another and things are far from straightforward and I'm not helping, I know that. It's just that I think I have to deal with life in bite-sized chunks at the moment and as you say Fiona McAllister has to come first.'

'Of course she does,' said Felicity.

'Will you give me a ring this evening when you get home?'

'You bet I will,' said Felicity, 'I want to hear all about Annabel Havers.'

'Oh right,' said Keith, 'so it's not because you want to hear the sound of my voice or anything like that?'

'Good lord no, Chief Inspector, I just want to make sure you're doing your job properly.'

They were back on an even keel.

20

Sydney Street had managed to maintain its Georgian elegance, despite the fact that most of the houses had been turned into flats. Not so for the Havers: they resided in some splendour in the whole of their house, the ground floor given over to a vast kitchen, dining room, play room and the first floor to an elegant drawing room into which Keith Penrose and his sergeant were shown by a cheerful Filipino lady who suggested coffee while they talked to her mistress.

Annabel Havers looked as though she had stepped straight out of the pages of *Vogue*. She was dressed rather formally in a powder-blue shift dress, a single string of pearls around her neck, her fair hair bobbed sleek and shiny. She was a good-looking woman who appeared younger than the mid-forties she had to be, as a contemporary of Moira's. She shook hands with both Keith and Jack, gesturing them to a large sofa by the fire place. Keith looked around him.

'You have a beautiful home here, Mrs Havers.'

'Yes I do,' Annabel agreed.

Despite the warmth of the greeting, instinctively there was something about this woman Keith did not like, a sense that she was play-acting at being the perfect hostess whereas, in reality, she couldn't wait to get rid of them.

'As my sergeant mentioned on the telephone, Mrs Havers, we are here about the death of Moira McAllister, formerly Moira Brown.'

'Yes, it was terrible,' said Annabel, 'I didn't realise for ages that it was the Moira I knew, I had lost touch with her before she married and had no idea of her new surname. It was only when I saw her picture in the paper that I realised who she was.'

'And you didn't think to contact the police?' Keith asked.

Annabel cast a cool gaze on him. 'I have nothing to tell you,' she said. 'I knew her once but that was years ago when we were both single. I am absolutely certain I have nothing useful to add to your investigations.'

'I'll be the judge of that,' said Keith, a little tersely.

The woman's superior attitude was already starting to grate. Jack, sensing this, took over. 'When did you and Moira first meet?' he asked.

'At university,' Annabel replied, 'we lived in

for the first year and had rooms opposite one another on the same corridor.'

'And after your first year?' Jack enquired.

'We had a house in Durham which we shared with two other students.'

'Girls?' Keith enquired.

'Yes.'

'Could I have their names?' Jack asked.

'Good heavens, umm ...' she hesitated. 'Elizabeth Bowen and Sarah Shankland.'

'Are you still in touch with them?' Keith asked.

'Not with either of them. Elizabeth married, I went to her wedding, she lives in the West Country somewhere, Devon I think, but we never meet, and poor Sarah ...' Her voice trailed away.

'Poor Sarah?' Keith asked.

'She died, it was tragic, she became a chalet girl and was killed in a skiing accident shortly after we all came down from university. It was a real shock at the time.'

'This Elizabeth Bowen,' Jack said, 'what is her married name?'

'Hardy, she is Elizabeth Hardy now. Come to think of it, I probably have her address and telephone number, would that be helpful?'

'It certainly would,' said Keith, 'thank you.'

The coffee arrived and while it was being poured Annabel crossed the room to her desk and produced a handsome leather-bound address book.

'Is your pen poised, sergeant?' she asked Jack.

'Absolutely,' he said.

'Elizabeth and Nicholas Hardy, they live in Tudor Cottage, St Germans ... oh Cornwall, not Devon, I've never been there myself, a bit of a trek.'

'A lovely little village, St Germans,' Keith said.

'Good heavens, do you know it?' Annabel replied.

'We're both from Cornwall,' Keith said, 'Devon and Cornwall Constabulary.'

'What on earth are you doing up here?' Annabel asked.

'You're probably aware from the papers that it is believed the McAllister murder is a copycat of one which took place nearly forty years ago. I was involved in that original case so I've been drafted in, hopefully to throw some light on the whole tragedy.'

'Do you really think both cases are linked?' Annabel said. There was no concern in her enquiry, Keith felt, only an idle, almost detached curiosity.

'We believe so,' he said. 'Can we return now to your relationship with Moira? I understand that as well as sharing a flat while at university you also shared a flat down here in London?'

Annabel nodded. 'Yes, Moira's parents were

dead and she had a flat in a block just across the King's Road from here.'

'In Chelsea Manor Street?'

'That's right,' said Annabel, 'she went there during the holidays from university and I visited her sometimes. My parents lived in a draughty pile up in Yorkshire in the middle of nowhere, so it was good to come down and visit Moira.'

'And when you left university?' Keith said.

'I became a permanent flatmate, I rented a room from Moira. We shared the flat for a couple of years.'

'And what did you do when you left university?'

'I didn't really want a career, not like Moira,' Annabel said, making it sound like a criticism, 'I worked in Brook Street, just off Bond Street almost opposite Claridges for some diamond importers, I was their receptionist – a really easy job,' she laughed. 'All I did was pour out gin and tonic and occasionally pick people up from Heathrow.'

'And then what happened?' Keith asked.

'We lived together for a couple of years and then, well, I left. We had a row.'

'May I ask what the row was about?' Keith asked.

'Well, it was over a man actually.'

There was a silence in the room. Obviously

Annabel felt that she had provided enough information.

'Who was the man and what happened?' Keith persisted.

'The man was my future husband, Christopher,' said Annabel. 'Moira had met him at a party, he was a baby banker in those days, they went out together for a couple of months and during that time Christopher and I started to realise ...' she hesitated, 'well, if you must know and to cut a long story short, Moira came home from work early one day and found Christopher and I ...' She shrugged her shoulders and walked over to the window, obviously finding the conversation difficult. 'There was a frightful row,' said Annabel, 'and Moira asked me to leave.'

'You make it sound as though she was being unreasonable?' Keith said.

'I think she was a little, I mean she and Christopher weren't all that close, they hadn't known each other long enough but she ordered me out of the flat there and then, literally, I had to pack my bags and go.'

'And have you seen her since?'

'No, never, she ordered me out of her flat and that was that, five years' friendship at an end.'

'Where did you go?' Keith asked.

'Oh, to Christopher's flat. We lived together

for a while and married about eighteen months later.'

'Did you invite Moira to the wedding?'

'You have to be joking!' said Annabel. 'As I say, we never saw each other again. She was so, so angry.'

For a moment both men were lost for words. It was clear that so far as Annabel was concerned, she had stolen Moira's boyfriend but seemed to think she was the victim.

'So,' said Keith, 'during the period you knew Moira, what did you know or learn about her background, her family and where she grew up?'

'Very little, next to nothing, she was a closed book in that department. She had no brothers and sisters and her parents had died.'

'How did they die?' Keith asked.

'A car crash, when she was in her teens. There was a solicitor who handled all the money for her, she was certainly never short of funds.'

'And friends, family friends, god-parents that sort of thing?'

'Nobody much, she was very dedicated to her work as I said and she had friends there. We had some friends mutually from university but she didn't like to talk about her family or her childhood and I respected that, it was all too painful was all she said.'

'No anecdotes, no mention of family holidays?'

Annabel was starting to get irritated. 'Inspector, I don't know how many different ways you want me to say this. I can tell you nothing about Moira's background, childhood or family – all I know about her began the day I met this girl who had a room opposite mine on the first day of our first term at university.'

'Didn't you think it odd?' Keith said, mirroring the question he had asked Ian McAllister.

'Not really, no, we were young; you live for the moment, don't you? Moira came and stayed with my family one summer for a few weeks, apart from that I don't think she would have known any more about me than I knew about her, it just wasn't relevant somehow.'

Briefly Keith wondered about his own children, was he no longer relevant now they were grown up? 'So there is nothing at all you can tell us about Moira's past that could help us in any way?'

Annabel frowned. 'I don't understand, poor Moira is dead, what has her past got to do with anything?'

'But you've read the papers?' said Keith, patiently.

'Yes.'

'So you know that Moira has now been identified as the sole survivor of the first murder forty years ago?'

'Yes, I understand,' said Annabel.

'And now there is a new missing little girl, Moira's daughter Fiona. If we could find out what happened to Moira during her childhood maybe we could find Fiona.'

'I see,' said Annabel, 'I'm sorry not to be able to help, but there really is nothing more I can tell you.'

'A bit of a cold fish,' Jack said, as they walked out onto the King's Road and started searching for a taxi.

'Poor old Moira,' says Keith, 'she loses her mother and her twin sister, she loses her identity and then she loses her boyfriend – no wonder she reacted as she did, keeping herself to herself. One loss too many, I would think.'

'I just didn't like the way Annabel was so uninvolved,' said Jack, 'so uncaring. If it had been a friend of mine who had been murdered, even if we had parted badly, I would still be affected by it, wouldn't you, sir?'

'Yes,' said Keith.

'Do you think we should interview the husband, Christopher?' Jack asked.

'No, not at this stage, I don't think,' Keith replied. 'Having left my card they know how to get hold of me. Presumably they will talk about it this evening. I think I will let them stew for a couple of days. I don't see them as materially involved in the case.' Seeing a taxi, Keith raised his hand and the taxi did a U-turn. 'Do you?' he asked Jack.

Jack shook his head. 'No.'

The two men spent what was left of the afternoon and evening at their hotel. They had turned Keith's room into a sort of incident room with a 'Do not disturb' notice on the door and they had papers strewn everywhere. By seven o'clock, none the wiser, they moved to the bar for a pint.

'Have you heard anything from the Met?' Jack asked.

'No, I think it is rather the other way around, I'm supposed to report to them.'

'Are you going to tell them about Annabel Havers?'

'I don't think so, there's not much point.'

'And Mrs Paradise, are you going to tell them that she believes the little girl wasn't present during the murders?'

Keith shook his head and smiled at Jack ruefully over the top of his pint. 'I'd be laughed at all the way back to Cornwall.'

'She is good at that sort of thing though, isn't she?' said Jack. 'We know that from first-hand experience.'

'Yes, but I don't see where it gets us.'

'I suppose,' said Jack, 'it could be that the killer intended the mothers to die but not necessarily the children.'

Keith shook his head. 'But why kill one child and leave the other alive, particularly in the case of twins?'

'Maybe Moira, alias Janey, wasn't there either like Fiona.'

'Possibly,' said Keith, 'but why, why, why? That's what we come around to every time.'

'So what next, sir?'

'I think we should go and see Elizabeth Hardy née Bowen,' said Keith.

'That's nothing to do with the fact that she lives in Cornwall, is it sir?' said Jack, with a ghost of a smile.

'Absolutely not,' said Keith, smiling back. 'I'm just hoping she might be able to give us a better slant on things, give us a bit more feel as to what Moira was like. She can't be more of a cold fish than Annabel Havers.'

'And from there?' said Jack.

'I think we go back to Truro and set up a proper incident room.'

'But if the Met can't solve it ...' Jack began.

'There is no reason why we shouldn't try, my boy,' said Keith.

In a village the size of St Germans it was not difficult to find Elizabeth Hardy. They had not rung ahead, and having taken a taxi from Plymouth station, they were relieved to find that she was at home. Tudor Cottage bore no relationship at all to the half-timbered, roses-around-the-door image that Keith had been expecting, but it was pleasing nonetheless – an old stone cottage beside a stream and a well-established orchard. It was a lovely day and having introduced themselves, Elizabeth suggested they had coffee in the garden. She was a small dumpy woman, with a round open face and ready smile; she could not have been in greater contrast to Annabel Havers. She had received no visits from the Met or anyone else and seemed surprised that the police should be interested in her long-ago relationship with Moira, but said she was happy to help in any way she could. She had read about it in the papers of course, and had been horrified when she had realised who it was. Settled around a wooden table by the stream Elizabeth seemed more than happy to talk.

'It is terrible,' she said, 'we four girls, me, Annabel, Moira and Sarah, terrible to think that two out of the four of us would not make old age and die so violently. Sarah, bless her, was only twenty-two when she died.'

'What can you tell me about Moira's character?' Keith asked.

'She was a very lonely buttoned-up sort of person, I think that was why she was friendly with Annabel because she was the exact opposite – so outgoing. Annabel used her rather as a stooge, I used to think. Moira was attractive but Annabel was beautiful and, how do I put this, women can be so bitchy sometimes, Chief Inspector, like ...' she thought for a moment, '... like beautiful brides often choose unattractive bridesmaids thinking the contrast will make them even more beautiful, it was rather like that with Annabel. I think she believed the contrast between her and Moira would make her stand out.'

'But as you say,' said Keith, 'Moira was not unattractive.'

'No, no she wasn't, a nice-looking girl but because she was so timid and quiet and Annabel so bouncy and confident ...' her voice trailed away, 'I don't know what I'm saying really.'

'I think I understand, she faded into the background rather,' said Keith. 'Did she talk about her family?'

'No, never, I never discussed it with her at all but Annabel told me that her parents had died in a car crash and she didn't want to talk about it. She had a flat in London and some solicitor who always coughed up money when she needed it. A couple of times we all ran out of rent money and the solicitor paid extra so we could keep the house.'

'Did she have interests, friends apart from you four?'

Elizabeth thought for a moment. 'Not really, she didn't play sport though she kept herself fit by jogging – that's a solitary occupation, isn't it?'

Keith nodded. 'So she didn't play an instrument in the local orchestra, or join the local dramatic society …'

'No, no, nothing like that. She read a great deal, she was an avid reader.' She smiled at Keith. 'Another thing best done alone. Come to think of it she was a bit of an enigma but you know what one is like at that age, so self-absorbed, I don't think anyone thought much about it. But surely her husband can help?'

'Not really,' said Keith, 'he is as much in the dark as the rest of you, and of course, they met when she was quite a lot older, fifteen years after you'd shared a flat with her, so her background, her childhood was less relevant. That is how he explained it and it makes sense.'

They talked a little about general things – Elizabeth's husband, David, was an estate agent in Plymouth, Elizabeth made pottery in a shed at the bottom of their garden, which was why they found her at home. They had no children, something Elizabeth said she regretted but it just wasn't to be, but it they seemed content with life.

'We are going to Truro tonight,' Keith said, in answer to Elizabeth's enquiry.

'How are you getting there?'

'We'll get a taxi back to Plymouth.'

'Oh, don't do that,' said Elizabeth, 'I'll give you a lift.'

'Are you sure?' Keith asked.

'Yes, no problem. It is an old Land Rover that has seen better days but it will get us there in one piece.'

Elizabeth chatted away cheerfully on the journey to Plymouth, but clearly she really had no more to tell them. At the station, having thanked her profusely, Keith handed over his card and scribbled his mobile number on the back.

'Anything, however trivial, that occurs to you please give me a ring, I don't mind how trivial it is, I don't mind what time of night or day you call me. We're desperately trying to find her daughter and maybe even the tiniest scrap of memory could help.'

21

It was good to be home, for that was how Jericho Cottage felt to Keith now. It had been early evening by the time he and Jack had reached Truro and Keith had decided that they would meet in his office early the following morning. Having indicated to Jack that he would be going home, in fact he had collected his car and driven straight to St Ives and to Felicity. They had supper and talked comfortably. Keith was unaccountably exhausted, the product he suspected of his mounting frustration. The missing child haunted him; he felt restless and irritable.

Felicity took it all in her stride. 'Why don't you have a bath or shower to relax you?' she said. 'I'll just take Harvey around the block and then an early night would do you no harm.'

'Sorry I'm such a grouch,' said Keith, 'I should offer to come with you ...'

'But you'd rather just stay here and brood,' Felicity finished for him with a smile.

'I think so, yes.'

After she had gone, Keith made himself another cup of coffee and sat down, head in his hands. He could see absolutely no way forward, that was the fact and while he failed to make any progress, that poor little girl … his mobile rang. He fished around in his pocket, it was a number he didn't recognise.

'Hello,' he said, 'Chief Inspector Penrose.'

'Oh, Inspector Penrose, it's Elizabeth Hardy, we spoke this morning.'

'Oh yes,' said Keith.

'I'm sorry to ring you so late but you did say any time.'

'I meant it, have you something more to tell me?' he said, his spirits rising slightly.

'It's only a little thing, but you said little things matter.'

'Yes, yes,' said Keith, trying to control his impatience.

'When she first came up to university she had a slight American accent.'

'An American accent?' Keith repeated.

'Yes, it was very slight, it was more intonation than pronunciation and by the time she left uni, she no longer had it. Certainly her husband wouldn't have considered her to have any kind of accent other than English. I don't know whether that's helpful?'

'Thank you,' Keith managed, 'thank you, yes I think it is.' He turned off his mobile and sat rock-still for a moment. Thomas Johnson lived in America. Had he been duped all along, was Thomas involved in the crimes and had he failed to spot it? He was so absorbed with his thoughts that he hardly heard the sounds of Felicity calling his name and thundering up the stairs.

'Keith, quick, that person who has been following me is outside, he is just down the street, I know he is, can you ...'

Quick as a flash Keith jumped up and was down the stairs. He ran out into the lane in time to see a figure detach itself from the shadows and head down towards the Wharf.

'Stop! Police!' he shouted. The figure quickened its pace but all Keith's pent-up frustration manifested itself in a dash down the lane. He caught the man just before he turned into Fore Street. 'Police,' he said again, grabbing him by the coat. The man put up no resistance; he was short and far from young, well into his fifties – he looked more embarrassed than anything else, certainly he did not look dangerous. 'You've been following Mrs Paradise, what is this all about?'

'I mean no harm,' the man said, 'I'm just doing my job.'

'And your job is?'

'I'm a private investigator, Robert Davies, Bob,' he said.

'And where have you come from, Mr Davies?' Keith asked.

'Bristol.'

'And may I ask why you are spying on Mrs Paradise?'

'I'm not a liberty to say, I am acting for my client.'

'Well, you can tell me now,' said Keith, 'or you can tell me at Truro police station, one or the other, and I've got all night so the decision is yours.'

'I'm not doing anything wrong,' Robert Davies said, defensively.

'You are, you're frightening a woman living alone for starters and I don't know who your client is but he can't be employing you in Mrs Paradise's best interests. Now tell me what is going on and tell me now or you are going to regret it. I've had a very harrowing week and I think I might be about to take it out on you, Mr Davies, unless you tell me what this is all about.'

'It is not he, it's a she,' said Bob Davies.

'OK, she,' said Keith, 'and who might she be?'

Bob Davies hesitated. 'You're Chief Inspector Keith Penrose?'

Keith nodded. 'Yes,' he said, slightly surprised.

'I don't like betraying client confidentiality, it's awkward you see.'

'Just tell me,' said Keith, clearly losing patience.

'Alright, I've been retained by your wife, Barbara. She wanted to know if you and Mrs Paradise were more than just friends,' he rallied a little, 'and I think I can probably tell my client that indeed you are, Chief Inspector.'

Keith climbed the stairs slowly to Felicity's kitchen and sat down heavily at the kitchen table.

'Well?' asked Felicity, nervously, 'did you get him, who is he, are you alright, did he hurt you?'

'He's harmless,' said Keith. He met her eye and she could see at once that something was terribly wrong.

'What is it?' she asked.

'He's a private investigator.'

'Investigator, investigating who, what?'

'Us,' said Keith. 'He is employed by Barbara.'

Twenty minutes later Keith was driving along the A30 towards Truro. Felicity had pleaded with him not to go but he was adamant. He needed to talk to Barbara, and Sydney was ten hours ahead. If he rang from home as soon as he got there at about half past ten, it would be half past eight in the morning in Sydney and he would be likely to find her at home.

'Is she gathering evidence for a divorce?' Felicity had asked.

'I just don't know,' said Keith, 'it's just so totally out of character. Normally, she is so up front, painfully so sometimes, this seems sneaky, underhand, it's not how she is. Like all of us she has got her faults but ...' he ran out of words.

'So she obviously knows about us,' Felicity said, in a small voice. 'How does that make you feel?'

'Damned angry,' said Keith, 'to have you frightened like this, it is so unnecessary. I sent him packing incidentally, he won't be back.'

'Good,' said Felicity, 'it has been horrible. I have tried not to worry you because you have so much going on at the moment, but I have to admit it has been scary.'

'Exactly,' said Keith, 'if she thought we were ...' he shrugged his shoulders, 'why didn't she just ask me?'

'You could turn that on its head,' Felicity suggested, 'you could say why on earth haven't you told her?'

Keith stared at Felicity. 'I don't know,' he said, 'you're right of course, I just don't like hurting people, I suppose I'm a coward and I'm certainly a thoughtless idiot for putting you through this. I can't understand why she put the chap outside *your* home. *I'm* the erring husband, why not have *me* followed?'

Felicity smiled in a vain attempt to lighten the mood. 'Come off it, Keith, she couldn't afford to have you followed, given your lifestyle, it would cost a fortune.'

'I suppose so,' Keith admitted grudgingly.

'And another thing,' said Felicity, 'Barbara may not know me but she does know you very well and I am sure she is certain that you would never take me to the family home, that really would be a betrayal in her eyes and yours. I would never come if you asked me, but I know you wouldn't and so does Barbara. That being the case, my home is the only point of contact to conduct an investigation into our relationship.'

Keith shook his head, ' I just can't believe she's done this.'

'Why don't you stay the night, you're exhausted. Tackle it in the morning.'

Keith shook his head. 'I'd never sleep, I need to find out why she did it and I need to find out now.'

He parked his car in the familiar driveway, for once not even glancing at the cathedral. He unlocked the front door, switched on the lights and went straight to the telephone. Barbara's number was still on the pad; he dialled it swiftly and waited.

'Hello,' she said.

'Barbara?'

'Yes, hello Keith, how are you? I wasn't expecting to hear again from you so soon, how is the case going?'

'Never mind the case, what on earth prompted you to employ a private investigator to stalk Felicity Paradise?'

There was a moment's silence.

'How on earth did you find out?'

'Barbara, I'm a policeman. He has been frightening the life out of Felicity, but tonight I caught him and some relatively mild bullying as to what I was going to do to him soon resulted in the name of his client. Why Barbara, why in God's name? If you thought I was having a relationship with Felicity Paradise, why not just ask?'

'Because you would have prevaricated, Keith, not for any bad reason but because you don't like hurting people, especially your family. You've got your faults like all of us, but I know the rest of us settling the other side of the world is very hard for you. Trying to decide what to do and how to do it and trying to please everyone must be driving you mad. I did it for you, Keith.'

'I don't understand,' said Keith, 'this is so unlike you, so out of character.'

'I'm trying to help,' said Barbara, firmly.

'How does that work?' Keith asked.

'I know moving to Australia isn't what you want, I know you can take the man out of Cornwall but not Cornwall out of the man, but I suspected there was another dimension to your difficulties and talking to Will one night he suggested to me that maybe you had become very close to Felicity Paradise. You may remember I asked you a couple of times about her while you were out here, hoping you might tell me what was going on but you wouldn't or couldn't, the latter I think, so I decided to find out for myself.'

'So that you can divorce me?' Keith asked.

'No, silly, so that I could tell you that I know and it's not a problem.'

'It's not?' said Keith, astounded.

'No, a lot of things have become clear to me since I moved out here, life is so much simpler and easier, more relaxed. Somehow ...' she hesitated, 'sorting out priorities doesn't seem to be such an issue. The whole time when we were married, we were stressed – you, of course, working all the time, me either raising children or working for the Council. People think living in Cornwall is an easy life, but it's not, it's just like everywhere else, just prettier.'

'I don't quite understand what you're saying,' said Keith.

'What I am saying is that all our married life I nagged you about your work, I resented it. I suppose, if I'm being honest, I was even envious of your involvement and sometimes of your triumphs, it must be wonderful to make a real difference when you get things right.'

'I think I've got it wrong more than I've got it right,' Keith suggested.

'I don't think so,' said Barbara, 'I think you are a very good policeman, I think you are wonderful at your job and I am so sorry that it has to end.'

Keith felt unexpectedly choked. 'Me too, I just don't understand your change of heart.'

'As I say,' said Barbara, 'it's being out here, putting some distance between life before Sydney and life now, having time to think. You weren't perfect, but neither was I. I never made enough allowances for the pressure you were under. Most work-related decisions that people have to make, might affect the balance sheet or the launch of a new product. If they get it wrong, it is not the end of the world. However, if you get it wrong and some villain goes free to kill or hurt again it can mean life or death. You've been down in the muck and bullets for so long, seen the worst of human nature and yet you still remained a nice person. That is no small achievement, Keith.'

'I don't know what to say,' Keith said.

'Then help me, help us both by answering truthfully, do you love Felicity Paradise?'

'Yes,' said Keith.

'Very much?'

'Yes, very much.'

'And does she love you?'

'Yes, yes I think so.'

'Think or know?'

'Know,' said Keith, after a moment.

'Then go to it lad, and be happy. I haven't had my report from Bob Davies yet but I gather he will tell me you've spent some time round there, and the only reason for getting him involved, I promise you, was so that I could find out what was really going on and give you my blessing.'

'I can hardly take this in,' said Keith.

'Why?' Barbara asked. 'Did you think I would go bananas when I found out?'

'Yes, I rather thought you would,' said Keith, 'that, and the kids would be appalled, and I'd end up losing you all.'

'You don't want to lose us, any of us?' Barbara asked.

'No, of course not, you're such an important part of my life, most of my life, I don't want to lose any of you and that includes you. It's a tall order, I know, but I want us to be friends, special friends.'

It was Barbara's turn to sound choked. 'Do you mean that?' she asked, in a slightly muffled voice.

'Of course I do,' said Keith, 'you can't go through what we've been through together and just throw it away. It was why I was so appalled by this private investigator. I assumed it was because you wanted to divorce me that we would have to go through some acrimonious, awful, damaging divorce process which would have destroyed the family. I just couldn't bear it.'

'Do you want to marry Felicity?' Barbara asked.

'I don't know,' said Keith, 'we haven't discussed it because we haven't finally decided that we're going to be together.'

'You mean she might not want that?'

'No,' said Keith, 'no, I think she wants that, I know she wants that, it was just me – I couldn't finally decide what to do – I was so torn.'

'She's been married, hasn't she?' said Barbara.

'Yes, for many years and has two children. Her husband was killed in a hit and run about eight years ago.'

'And she has been alone ever since?'

'Yes,' said Keith.

'If you two want to marry that's fine with me,' said Barbara.

'Barbara, I don't understand, why are you being so generous? No, that sounds wrong, it sounds like I don't expect you to be generous. I suppose I can't imagine any wife being happy about her husband remarrying – certainly not in my experience.'

'Ours has never been the most passionate of relationships, has it? No blame, it's just a fact, even at the beginning. I think passion and jealousy go hand in hand, I'm not jealous of Felicity, Keith, because I can't see a future for us together, but I like the idea of special friends. Tell me, what will you do with the house, I presume you don't want to live there?'

'If she'll have me,' said Keith, 'I rather thought I would go and live in St Ives, sell the house and split the proceeds.'

'That would be a good retirement project for you,' said Barbara. 'There are a number of items I'd like sent out to Australia and the rest you can either have or can be sold. With the mortgage paid off and our respective pensions, the sale of the house should make us pretty comfortably off.'

'It would be nice to help the children a little,' Keith suggested.

'I thought that, so let's sell everything and before we split it give the children each something depending on how much we manage to sell the house for?'

'Yes,' Keith said, 'if we give it to them before

we split the proceeds then it would be a joint gift, which would be a nice way to do it.'

'While ours hasn't been the most perfect of marriages, Keith,' Barbara said, 'we did get something right with those two children.'

'We certainly did,' said Keith.

'They are both so happy out here and Will is so settled compared to how he has been, it is marvellous to see. You go and straighten things out with your Felicity Paradise and then let's put everything on hold until you retire.'

'I can't believe we are having this conversation,' said Keith, 'it feels unreal.'

'But good?' Barbara asked.

'Oh yes, very good. Thank you, thank you so much for understanding.'

'I understand, Keith, I'm just sorry it's taken me a while. We'll be in touch.'

Keith replaced the receiver and sat very still by the hall table for a moment or two, then he stood up and walked to the kitchen. Without really knowing what he was doing, he plugged in the kettle and realising there was no milk, made himself a black coffee. Then he went into the sitting room and sat down in what had been known as Dad's chair. All through his career he had been told he was good with people and he had come to believe it, but never in a million years would he have imagined the conversation he had just had with his wife was possible. He thought he would have known exactly how Barbara would react to the revelation of his relationship with Felicity.

He had imagined recriminations: how she had given him the best years of his life and now he was retiring, he was off with someone else, how ungrateful etc, etc. Instead, not only had she welcomed his relationship with Felicity, she had actually helped him to make the decision. Maybe it had set her free too in a strange way – he wondered for a moment whether there was someone in her life, but he thought not, he thought probably she just wanted to be free of a tired marriage to a workaholic policeman, she was ready to move on.

It was extraordinary, he felt shocked to the core but at the same time a huge weight had been lifted, the relief was almost tangible. He finished his coffee and glanced at his watch. It was now nearly one o'clock in the morning, he should be exhausted but he knew sleep was a long way off. He washed up his cup and left it to drain, then without a backward glance, he locked the front door, climbed into his car and headed for St Ives, Jericho Cottage and Felicity Paradise.

22

Five hours later Felicity was standing in front of the Aga brewing coffee and whipping up scrambled eggs. Below her she could hear Keith whistling tunelessly in the shower and the thought that this was what she would hear most mornings of her life to come filled her with a joy she could hardly bear. They had slept very little, talking through plans, remaking them, marvelling at the magnificence of Barbara's gesture. And it was magnificent – it was not just a gift to Keith, it was a gift to Felicity too, she realised. Annie's criticism of her relationship with Keith had hurt so much because she knew that a lot of what Annie had said was true. The concept of trying to be happy at the expense of someone else's unhappiness was a tough one to reconcile. Over the years it had been a constant source of amazement to Felicity to see friends go in and out of marriages, leaving behind appalling unhappiness and destruction and yet seeming to move on to a new relationship without any apparent guilt. If their relationship, hers and Keith's, had caused Barbara deep unhappiness it would have been hard to see how their love could have blossomed and deepened to last the rest of their lives, it would have been tainted somehow. As it was, Barbara had set them free, not reluctantly, not at Keith's request: it had been *her* decision, *her* initiative. Keith had always intimated that she was a strong woman, and she certainly had to be that. What a gift she had given them.

'Breakfast is ready,' she called down to Keith.

'Coming,' he said, bounding up the stairs. He looked a different man this morning despite the lack of sleep. He was wearing a blue striped shirt and grey suit trousers and was fiddling with his tie as he took his place at the breakfast table, his hair still damp from the shower.

Felicity stared at him for a moment. I can't believe he is mine, she thought.

'What are you staring at?' he asked with a smile.

'I was just thinking what a fine figure of a man you are, Chief Inspector.'

'Now, none of that,' he said, 'I cannot be late for work this morning.'

She grinned at him. 'I've done you some eggs, you hardly touched your supper last night.'

'Brilliant, thanks. I never got a chance to tell

you last night, with everything that happened.' He took a sip of coffee and began attacking his eggs. 'One of Moira's old flatmates reckons she had an American accent, just a slight one, when she first went up to university.'

'Goodness,' said Felicity, sitting down opposite him. 'What does that mean?'

'Well, it could mean that Thomas Johnson is involved in some way, but how I'm not sure, not yet.'

'The man you went to see in Washington, the father of Moira?'

'Adoptive father, yes, actually uncle in reality.'

'But I thought you really liked him, thought he was a decent bloke?'

'I do, I did, I'm just starting to wonder if I've been had.'

When Keith arrived at the office he went straight upstairs and made an appointment with Brenda, George Staple's secretary.

'I only need five minutes,' he said.

'Come back in half an hour then, Keith, I'll fit you in.'

'Thanks, Brenda, you're a star.'

Downstairs he found Jack who had managed to secure a small, rather airless office they could use as an incident room. Jack eyed him and then allowed himself a broad grin.

'What?' Keith asked.

'You look a lot better sir, this morning, if I may say so.'

'Better than what?' Keith asked.

'Better than you have been in a long while. Am I allowed to know why?'

'Certainly not,' said Keith, 'and you have a lot to do this morning. Something has happened, something which could be significant.'

Jack assumed a serious expression. He knew perfectly well what had put the smile back on his boss's face but he would hold his counsel for now.

'Could you ring Annabel Havers and ask her whether she remembers Moira having a slight American accent when she first went up to university?'

'Blimey,' said Jack, 'where did that idea come from?'

'It isn't an idea,' said Keith, 'Elizabeth Hardy rang me last night. We had asked her to think of any small detail and she came up with that. It could be very important.'

'Meaning?' said Jack.

'Meaning that Moira could have spent her childhood in America.'

'And?' said Jack.

'Look, one thing at a time, if you could make

that call and when you've asked her the question could you also ring Ian McAllister and ask him whether he ever spotted a trace of an American accent. Elizabeth says it was more intonation than anything.'

Jack frowned.

'Come on Jack, get focused, Americans put the emphasis in a different place from us on some words.'

'Oh right,' said Jack, 'I'm on to it sir. What are you doing?'

'I'm off to see George Staple, I'll fill you in when I get back.'

George stood up when Keith came into the room and came around from behind his desk to shake Keith's hand.

'How's it going, Keith?'

'It wasn't going very well but I think I might have had a bit of a breakthrough, though it's a straw in the wind to be honest, sir.'

'Come and sit down,' said George.

'It's about Moira McAllister alias Janey Johnson, who if you remember dropped back onto our radar screen as a fully-formed eighteen-year old having been missing for eleven years. We learnt last night that at eighteen she had a slight American accent, no one has ever mentioned that before.'

'And so you are suggesting that she was raised for part of her childhood in the States?'

'Not just the States, I'm thinking Thomas Johnson.'

'He's the man you went to see in Washington?'

'That's right.'

'I thought everybody believed him to be entirely innocent. He was in Washington when the first murder happened, wasn't he?'

'Yes he was,' said Keith, 'but I'm beginning to think he is involved in this somehow, I think he deliberately led me on a false path. I liked the man but there has been a niggle going on in the back of my mind ever since I returned from Washington and now this latest piece of information makes me think – well, I think I allowed myself to be manipulated.'

'So what do you want me to do?' said George.

'Can you get hold of the police department in Washington and find me someone of a similar rank to mine who I can talk to and who can make things happen?'

'You're not going to have Thomas Johnson arrested, are you, not on such flimsy evidence?'

'No, no, nothing like that, not at this stage.'

'I'll see what I can do for you,' said George, 'I'll come back to you with a name and a number. I imagine you don't want me to run this past the

Met?'

'No, thank you sir,' said Keith, smiling. He rose to go and George rose with him.

'How are you feeling about everything, your retirement I mean specifically?'

'Alright,' said Keith, 'only because I haven't had a chance to think about it, I'm too preoccupied with this little girl.'

George smiled. 'Nothing much changes with you, does it, Keith?'

'It's about to though, isn't it?' Keith said, sadly.

Back in the incident room Jack was waiting for him.

'Two interesting things, sir, I spoke to Annabel Havers first and she confirms that Moira did have a slight American accent when they first met. I tried to be subtle about it, I didn't ask her the question outright, I just said had there been a trace of any accent when Moira and she had first met and she confirmed straight away that there had been and it was American.'

'Good,' said Keith, 'and what about Ian McAllister?'

'No accent, she sounded entirely English by the time they met but he did say that she was reluctant to ever go to America. There was some conference they could have attended together and she wouldn't go. The reason she gave was that she had been to America once with her parents and had hated it and didn't want to go back, which seems a bit weak.'

'Interesting,' said Keith. 'Do you know, Jack, I think we might be starting to make a bit of progress, and not before time.'

While they waited for George Staple to come up with a name, Keith and Jack talked through the implications of the latest developments.

'Supposing Thomas Johnson resented the fact that Caroline would not move to Washington with him, thus depriving him of his daughters. Bear in mind,' Keith continued, pacing up and down the floor, 'that Caroline was no blood relation to the girls, and it may well be that Thomas thought he was entitled to them since they were his nieces by blood. Supposing his intention had been to kill Caroline and bring the girls out to the States but something went wrong and poor little Katie was killed by mistake.'

'But he didn't murder Caroline, did he?' said Jack. 'He had a cast-iron alibi, he was in Washington.'

'But he could have hired a hit man.'

'I know I am a naïve Cornish boy, sir,' said Jack, 'but is that really likely?'

'I think it possibly is,' said Keith, 'he certainly

had the money.'

'OK,' said Jack, 'so he hires a hit man to come over, murder his wife and presumably kidnap his two daughters and bring them out to America. Why did he do that, why not just apply through the courts? He was the blood relation.'

'He couldn't, could he,' said Keith, 'because he didn't have any legal right to them, neither he nor Caroline did. Caroline was told she couldn't have children about the same time the twins were born, they began taking care of them and then when Thomas's sister died they simply kept the girls.' Keith thumped his forehead. 'Idiot, why they didn't apply to adopt them then? They were the obvious candidates. I don't imagine there would have been any problem, they had been caring for them, the girls had presumably already bonded with them and Thomas was their uncle.'

'Maybe,' said Jack, 'there was a reason why one or both of them wouldn't have been eligible as adoptive parents.'

'Exactly,' said Keith. 'Why didn't I think of it before? There has to be a skeleton in their cupboard!'

'We could start searching, though it's not going to be easy after all this time,' Jack said.

'Jack, when has this case ever been easy?' said Keith, tiredly. 'Just do it, old lad, would you? See what you can find.'

'It was more than forty years ago.'

'I know.'

'Are you sure it wasn't done at the time?'

'I'm not,' Keith admitted. 'I tell you what, why don't you have a word with Graham Sinclair and ask him if he still has the background details on the Johnsons and if so, whether you could have access to criminal records for the period they were growing up?'

'Does this mean another trip to London?' Jack said, tiredly.

'It might,' said Keith, 'or you never know, Graham might help you.'

'Help us – I thought you had fallen out with him?' Jack asked.

'I have rather, but you haven't. Explain that you are my sergeant and that I've authorised you to investigate this.'

'What if he asks how we're getting on?' Jack asked.

'Tell him nothing,' said Keith.

'Are you sure?' said Jack.

'Quite sure.'

23

The time difference meant that George Staple was unable to reach the Washington police department until two o'clock UK time. It was after four o'clock therefore before Keith had a name – Police Chief Danny Salsburg. Keith called him straight away and introduced himself.

'Hi Keith,' said Danny, 'I've been waiting for your call, it sounds an interesting case, your boss has filled me in a little. What do you want us to do, do you want us to arrest this Thomas Johnson guy and rattle his cage a little?'

'Absolutely not,' said Keith, 'not yet anyway. Bearing in mind it could involve the kidnap of a child we need to tread very carefully.'

'Jeez, I hadn't realised a kid was involved. How old?'

'A little girl, her name is Fiona McAllister, she is seven.'

'An English kid?'

'Yes,' said Keith.

'And you reckon this guy has got her, is he a relation?'

'A sort of grandfather,' said Keith, 'he is actually a great uncle but he looked after Fiona's mother as a daughter, at least we think he may have done. This is where I need you to help.'

'OK, shoot,' said Danny.

'Firstly can you establish whether Thomas Johnson has a holiday home anywhere? You have his address in Washington, I take it?'

'Yeah,' said Danny.

'OK, that is just a small apartment and it wouldn't be suitable for a child so we're looking to see if he has another property anywhere. Can you dig around?'

'Certainly can, anything else?'

'Yes, it may be he raised a child before, forty-odd years ago. She was another little seven-year-old and her name was probably Moira, but not definitely, it could have been Janey.'

'Keith, if you don't mind me saying so, this case is getting mighty weird.'

'I'm sorry,' said Keith, 'I want to explain it to you properly but we haven't got time now, there is this child to consider.'

'Right, got that,' said Danny. 'Anything else?'

'Yes, can you check out whether this Thomas Johnson has any kind of criminal record, anything that would make it difficult to adopt a child. We are also trying to establish whether he has any criminal record here. He started life as an Englishman but forty years ago he moved to Washington and ultimately took American citizenship. I think any criminal record is more likely to have occurred here in this country which might be why he moved to the States.'

'But surely if his application for American citizenship had thrown up any problem, he would have been sent back home? We're very choosy, you know.'

Keith laughed. 'I am sure you are, and quite right too. Yes, that is a good point but could you check in any event?'

'Will do, how do I reach you?'

Keith gave him all his numbers.

'We need no expense spared on this, time is critical. I am sure the Met will pick up any bills you incur.'

'If there is a little girl's life at stake here, this is not a problem. Things are pretty quiet at the moment, I will give it top priority and I'll be back to you within twenty-four hours, I promise.'

A dejected Jack received little cooperation from Graham Sinclair.

'I am travelling up on the sleeper tonight,' he told

Keith. 'I'm being thrown into the dusty archives of the Met. Graham says he has no spare people to put on the job at the moment.'

'What, not even for a missing child?'

'Apparently not,' said Jack. 'I get the strange feeling that you are not flavour of the month, sir.'

'You are probably right,' said Keith, 'I'm sorry. How is Maggie taking it?'

'Not that well, but she is remaining relatively cooperative because of your impending retirement.'

'Oh great,' said Keith, 'she'll be glad to see the back of me.'

'No, no,' said Jack, 'she's actually gutted you're retiring and to be honest, she's not that teasy.'

'Well, thank her for me will you?' said Keith. 'I'm off home now.'

'Are you, sir?' said Jack, smiling.

'What's that supposed to mean?' Keith asked.

'Nothing, I will call you tomorrow as soon as I get anywhere.'

'Thanks, Jack,' said Keith.

'I think Jack has worked out what is going on between you and me,' Keith said, later that evening. They'd had supper and Keith was sitting hunched over his notebook while Felicity washed up.

'Do you mind?' she asked.

'No,' he said, 'we'll have to tell everyone soon enough, I suppose.'

'Not before the children,' said Felicity, 'all of them. How do you think yours will react?'

'I think they will take their cue from Barbara,' said Keith. 'I know we will have no problem with Will, it's only Carly really to worry about. As we have her mother's blessing, I can see no real objection coming from Carly. What about yours?'

Felicity dried her hands then turned around to face him, smiling. 'We will have no problem at all with Martin, he thinks a great deal of you, as you know.'

'And I of him,' said Keith.

'I think Jamie will be OK once he is confident that you are not going to love and leave me, he is quite protective where his mother is concerned.'

'He needs to have no worries on that score,' said Keith. He stood up and took Felicity in his arms. 'As you well know, but that brings us to Mel.'

'Ah, Mel,' said Felicity.

'This is sounding tricky,' said Keith.

'I'm not sure,' said Felicity, 'I love her, she is my daughter, I would step into the cannon's mouth for her any day of the week.'

'I can feel a "but" coming,' said Keith.

'There *is* a "but". She is quite self-centred, she likes everything to go her way. That is why Martin is so perfect for her, he bumbles along in her wake without any resentment and to be fair, without Mel's get-up-and-go, I doubt he would ever have got his market garden off the ground, so it works well both ways. Nonetheless she likes to be the centre of attention and,' Felicity smiled, 'she likes to have a free babysitter. She'll work out I might not be so available when I'm part of a couple.'

'That's a bit selfish,' said Keith.

'Come on, Keith, one of the things we have to agree on is never to criticise each other's children.'

'True,' Keith agreed, 'I would be furious if you criticised Carly.'

'There you go then. Mel is what she is, just like we are, an individual with good points and bad and maybe I am making an unnecessary fuss. She may be thrilled to bits that somebody else is going to take on her mother in her old age.'

'Who says anything about old age?' said Keith. 'I am simply toying with you until I can find a younger model.'

Felicity swiped him with a tea towel and they ended up in each other's arms again.

'I can tell that you are really worried tonight,' Felicity said after a while.

'I am,' said Keith, 'can I tell you all about it?'

'Coffee?'

'Yes please, tons of it.' He resumed his seat at

the table. 'I did have one success today which was to persuade the "Super" to put me in touch with the Washington Police Department. I have a contact – a Police Chief Danny Salsburg, he is finding out at his end what he can about Thomas Johnson.'

'So what is your current theory?' Felicity asked.

'I think Thomas Johnson could have brought Moira up in America and then posted her into Durham University with money to live on and a new identity, ie. Moira Brown, and that is why we can find no trace of Moira before she attended university.'

'Is he rich enough to have been able to do that?' said Felicity. 'I am sorry to be so practical and basic but these things matter.'

'Of course they do,' said Keith. 'Yes, without a doubt, he is a very wealthy man, I would say. A full set of papers are not that expensive and with no other dependents, I would have thought setting her up in a flat in London with a generous allowance would be well within his means.

'So he never remarried?'

'Not as far as I know,' said Keith, 'certainly he was living a bachelor existence when I met him a couple of weeks ago. The question is not so much how he did it, which is quite feasible, the question is why?'

Felicity sat down at the table opposite Keith

and frowned at him.

'Thomas Johnson was the twins' father for practical purposes, but biologically he was their uncle, right?'

'Yes,' said Keith.

'And the mother had no biological relationship at all with the children?'

'Again correct,' said Keith.

'So if the mother refused to go to Washington with Thomas when he landed this prestigious job in America's capital then he could have been, well, fed up with the concept of his wife holding onto children that weren't biologically hers but were biologically his and refusing to join him.'

'All true, my thoughts exactly,' said Keith. 'And in fairness to Caroline it might not simply have been that she didn't want to go to America, or was being pig-headed for some reason. It could have been that as there was no legal adoption in place for the children, she would be worried that they might have been taken away from them. They would have needed to demonstrate a legal adoption for them to have got passports and visas to travel to the States. Maybe it was a risk she simply wasn't prepared to take.'

'That makes sense,' said Felicity. 'The girls were seven at the time of the murders, like Fiona?'

'Seven, yes,' said Keith, 'imagine raising two

children for seven years and then facing the prospect of losing them? I can't believe they would have lost them, but that is what Jack is checking out now, whether there is any criminal record or stain on either of their characters which might have made adoption difficult. Thomas said they never bothered adopting the children because they felt there was no need, but it might not be that simple, maybe there was a reason for it.'

'So,' said Felicity, 'Thomas Johnson is in Washington and his wife and daughters are in London and you are completely convinced that his alibi for the night of the murders is cast iron?'

'Absolutely,' said Keith, 'we checked, rechecked and triple-checked. There is no way he could have been in London in order to kill his wife.'

'But he could have hired somebody to do it, did you look at that?'

'No,' said Keith, 'we were so convinced that he was innocent, I still find it hard to see him as a killer.'

'Why?' Felicity asked.

'I don't know, he just comes across as a regular guy and I'm normally a reasonable judge of character. When I was with him around the period of the murders he seemed so genuinely distressed and bewildered by the awful things that had happened to them, it never occurred to me that he could be making it all up.' After a moment of silence, Keith said. 'So why was the other twin killed then, poor little Katie?'

'Maybe it was an accident,' said Felicity, 'Maybe Katie tried to save her mother, maybe Thomas meant to raise both girls but Katie got in the way.'

'So what was Janey doing? At the time we were confident that both girls were in the house. Caroline had picked them both up from school, they had been seen on the way home.'

'Unless,' said Felicity, 'it was something terribly simple.'

'Like what?' said Keith.

'Janey was in the garden or watching television upstairs.'

'So the hit man takes Janey and spirits her off to Washington while PC Plod and his useless sergeant are bumbling around the house looking for clues. With a pre-booked flight it wouldn't have taken long to get from Fulham to Heathrow, particularly forty years ago when traffic wasn't so heavy.'

'What time of day was it?'

'Early evening.'

'So the bulk of the rush hour would have gone and they could have been at Heathrow quite quickly.'

'We checked flights but if the flight was pre-booked in the name of the hitman and the two little girls with false identities we could have missed it,' said Keith, 'you're right.'

'So what happens next?' Felicity asked.

'My opposite number in Washington is trying to establish whether there was ever a child in Thomas Johnson's life and Jack is trying to establish whether there was any reason why it might have been difficult for Caroline and Thomas to adopt the girls.'

'And in the meantime?' Felicity asked.

Keith let out a sigh and smiled faintly at her. 'We wait.'

24

Keith spent another morning waiting for news. The temptation to ring Thomas Johnson direct and ask him why his daughter had acquired an American accent was almost overwhelming, but of course he resisted it. He only had to think of the danger such a call might put little Fiona in, to make such a confrontation quite impossible. Instead he tried to concentrate on the McAllister murder and to attempt to put together a case as to why Thomas should have been involved in both murders. Why would a man kill a daughter he had raised so carefully, having taken so much trouble and care? It made no sense. Why kill her and why kill her son, his grandson? The improbability of Thomas being involved in this second murder made Keith look again at the conclusion he had jumped to so readily on hearing that Moira had an American accent. Was he on a wild goose chase, was he concentrating his efforts exclusively on Washington when in fact he should be looking closer to home? It was a faint trace of an American accent, Elizabeth Hardy had said. Maybe this could have been acquired by living with Americans who weren't even necessarily based in America. Why had this case come back to haunt him again and why did he seem no nearer to solving it than he had done forty years ago? Just when he was close to despair, shortly before two o'clock in the afternoon, Jack rang.

'I think I might have the reason why Thomas Johnson was reluctant to go through the formal adoption channels.'

'Go on,' said Keith, his heart racing.

'Thomas Johnson went to a public school in Wiltshire, he was a good student and did well but he got into trouble after he had finished what was then called School Certificate.'

'I know all about exams,' said Keith with feeling.

'After he had finished his exams, there was a girl, she was the daughter of one of the school's housemasters, she had a fearful reputation for promiscuity, it was known she was certainly no virgin which was unusual in a sixteen-year-old in those days, I believe.'

'We were all as pure as driven snow,' said Keith, 'get on with it, please Jack.'

'Sorry, sir. She went on a picnic to celebrate the end of exams with three boys and then alleged they gang-raped her. One of those boys was Thomas Johnson.'

'What happened?' said Keith.

'Well, not a lot, it was before DNA, remember. She was known to be sexually very active and she had no bruises, her clothes weren't torn, and she did not seem particularly traumatised. The general feeling is that she had become fed up with the boys or had a row with them and made up the story in part, at any rate, to get them into trouble.'

'So is that really enough to make Thomas Johnson nervous?' Keith asked.

'He was formally charged, all three boys were, and after a week or so the charges were dropped. The cold case guys here are really helpful. I've been talking it through with one of them, his view is that as well as there being insufficient evidence to make the charges stick the school would not have been keen for the charges to be made with all the resulting publicity. She was a naughty girl and in those days rape was not treated as seriously.'

'So what happened to the boys?'

'They were expelled but, being a very bright boy, in the case of Thomas Johnson he did his A levels at Harrow, and from there went on to Oxford.'

'If no charges were made,' said Keith, 'surely there would have been no problem, no blemish on his record?'

'Maybe not,' said Jack, 'certainly it didn't prohibit Thomas from taking American citizenship, but maybe the search into his background for the purposes of adoption may have been more thorough. There was a lot of publicity about it at the time and it made the headlines for some days, it wasn't that difficult to find.'

'Well, thanks, Jack, that is really helpful.'

'There's something else, sir,' said Jack, sounding pleased with himself.

'Well, spit it out, lad,' said Keith, irritably.

'While I was researching Thomas Johnson's background, I found something very interesting.'

'Oh for heaven's sake, what?'

'Thomas's mother's name was Moira. Now if I was going to re-christen my daughter, calling her after her granny seems like a good idea to me.'

Keith sat back in his chair and gave a great sigh. 'I think you might have cracked it,' he said.

'Can I come home now?'

You certainly can,' said Keith, 'well done.'

The temporary euphoria created by Jack's news burst like a bubble twenty minutes later when Keith received a phone call from Graham Sinclair.

'Are you holding out on me, Keith?' he asked without any preamble.

'No,' said Keith, 'to be honest I am revolving

in confused circles at the moment. Have there been any developments your end?'

'None worth speaking of,' Graham admitted. 'I pointed your sergeant in the direction of finding out as much as he could about Thomas Johnson and I gather he has turned up a bit of bother.'

'Yes, not much to go on though,' said Keith.

'Would you mind me asking why you are so interested in Thomas Johnson's background suddenly?'

'We spoke with one of Moira McAllister's flatmates,' said Keith, 'who mentioned that when she first met Moira she had a slight American accent. It made me wonder whether Thomas Johnson was actually involved in his wife's and daughter's murder.'

'He had an alibi.'

'I realise that,' said Keith, 'I was there, remember.'

'No need to be so touchy, Keith. The girl could have had an American accent for all sorts of reasons.'

'This is true,' said Keith, 'it was just a thought.'

'You'll keep me up to speed, won't you, if anything develops? Time is running out for this little girl.'

'I will,' said Keith, and replaced the receiver. Should he have told Graham Sinclair about his contact with the States? Not really, it wasn't going to help in any way at the moment. If the whole enquiry shifted towards Thomas Johnson and if in fact he had got things wrong, then valuable police time would have been wasted on a hiding to nothing. Better that he went off on a tangent of his own, assuming that is what it was. He tried to concentrate on some paperwork but kept glancing at the phone. At about half past four it rang.

'It's only me,' said Felicity.

'Oh,' said Keith.

'Fantastic response,' said Felicity, 'it is so nice to know I am appreciated.'

'You are appreciated, my love,' he said, 'I was just hoping you might be Danny, the policeman from Washington.'

'I know, I know, only joking,' she said. 'I've been thinking about you all day and I thought I would ring to see how it was going. Any news?'

'No,' said Keith, 'not really. We found a bit of form on Thomas Johnson, an alleged rape when he was a schoolboy, but it is all fairly nebulous, but it could just have accounted for why he didn't want to go through the adoption process, and we have learnt that Thomas's mother was called Moira.'

'Interesting … I've been thinking,' said Felicity, 'supposing Janey/Moira didn't realise her mother and sister had been murdered, supposing she didn't find out about it until she came to university in England, supposing when she did find out and she put two and two together and realised that her father had been responsible, maybe she was blackmailing him or simply threatening to inform the police. That could be a motive for murder. We have to assume that the man is unhinged anyway.'

'He doesn't seem unhinged,' said Keith.

'People went on getting shaved and having haircuts from Sweeney Todd for decades without realising they ran the risk of being turned into a pie. There are a lot of seriously crazy people out there who don't present as mad.'

'I know. There's no need to tell me,' said Keith.

'Apart from unloading my latest brilliant theory,' said Felicity, 'I was also ringing to ask whether you were in for supper tonight.'

'I'm going to hang on here for a while to see if Danny rings me, but yes please. Shall we say eight, eight-thirty?'

He had hardly replaced the receiver when the phone rang again.

'Is that Keith? Danny Salsburg here.'

'Any news?' said Keith.

'Yes, a bit. You were right, he does have a holiday home on Cape Cod, Atlantic side, fairly well down, not the smartest part which is strange.

Given his address here in Washington I'd have imagined he would have been amongst all the picket fences.'

'I'm not really familiar with Cape Cod,' Keith said.

'The further down you go the rougher it gets.'

'OK,' said Keith, 'is there any news on the daughter?'

'Not yet. We have established that no little girl was registered at any schools here in Washington. I've got people working on it down in Cape Cod now. I take it you still don't want us to go and visit him?'

'No, absolutely not but please Danny, I know it is a long shot expecting schools to have records that are forty years old, but if we can find anything, it would be a huge help.'

'You know you are a funny lot you, Brits. I just don't see what the problem is here – if you suspect the man may have kidnapped the little girl, why are we messing about trying to link him to a forty year-old crime? If you think he is connected to the current one, let's go see. I have no jurisdiction in Massachusetts but I know a good guy there. If you want to go out and join him I am sure there would be no problem. This Thomas Johnson is a Brit, right?'

'I think he has dual nationality,' said Keith, 'he

was born in England but he spent most of his life working in Washington.'

'OK, a mongrel. Let's just do it, Keith. Why not get on a plane, come out here and we'll sort this guy out. I don't like people messing with little girls. I'll fix it, get a plane to Boston and I'll have you met there.'

Keith slowly replaced the receiver and rang the switchboard.

'Is the "Super" still there?' he asked.

'He's just left.'

Keith glanced at his watch; it was four minutes after five. George Staple was very much a creature of habit. Unless there was a flap on, he would now be on his way out of the building. Keith caught up with him in the car park.

'I want to go to Boston, sir,' he said.

'When?' George asked.

'Well, now.'

'Have they got something on Thomas Johnson?'

'Not really,' said Keith.

George leaned on the roof of his car. 'What does "not really" mean, Keith?'

'We have established that he has a holiday home in a rather remote part of Cape Cod.'

'And?' said George Staple.

'And nothing.'

'So you reckon on the strength of that information he has murdered his daughter and kidnapped his granddaughter? It is not against the law, Keith, to have a holiday home.'

'I know,' said Keith. 'I know this is a wild hunch. Look, I will pay for my own flight, I just need your permission to go.'

'What do they think over there?'

'They are all for me coming out, they think it is worth a punt. They are trying to establish whether Moira attended school out there, but we are looking at records that are forty years old. It was Danny Salsburg's suggestion that I should come out, that we should stop messing and see if we can find Fiona. If I am wrong about all this, I will have egg on my face, but if I am right, we still may be able to save her.'

George gave Keith a searching look. 'Do you truly believe that Thomas Johnson could be involved in these murders?'

Keith met his gaze. 'To be absolutely frank, sir, I really, really do not know.'

'That's good enough for me,' said George Staple. 'Go and book your flight, look on it as a retirement present.'

'Thank you sir. Oh, and by the way, Thomas's mother was called Moira.'

'Well, that does it then, Keith, an open and

shut case,' said George with the trace of a smile.

Keith was quite incapable of booking the flight online, so he hurried upstairs to where he found Brenda, George Staple's secretary, just packing up.

'Can you do me a favour?' he asked. Twenty minutes later he was booked on an early morning flight to Boston. If he set off now and drove most of the night he could just about make it. With Brenda's help he e-mailed Danny Salsburg telling him he was taking his advice, and giving details of his flight. Then he picked up his briefcase and went down to the car park; once in his car he dialled Felicity's number.

'About that supper …' he began.

25

Faced with an evening alone, Felicity rang Martin and Mel. Martin answered.

'Have you had supper yet?' Felicity asked.

'No,' said Martin, 'we're just beating the kids into submission. Bath-time has been particularly messy tonight.'

'Instead of cooking,' said Felicity, 'why don't I come over and babysit and you and Mel go out to dinner? I've just had a cheque from my publishers and I would like to treat you.'

'That is terribly kind,' said Martin, 'but I think it is a truly appalling idea. What I would like you to do is come over here and have supper with us and put your hard-earned cheque towards something spoiling for yourself.'

'Wouldn't you like a quiet evening on your own?'

'No,' said Martin, 'we'd like a quiet evening with you. If you absolutely insist, you can bring a bottle.'

As they sat over the remains of their supper, drinking wine and nibbling on some cheese, Felicity knew it was the right moment. There would never be a better one.

'The thing is,' she said, 'I haven't told Jamie yet, but I am sort of involved with a man.'

'Your policeman, I assume?' said Mel, in a none-too friendly voice.

'Yes,' said Felicity, 'how did you know?'

'Oh for heaven's sake, Mother, we've known for ages, it's so obvious.'

'Is it?' said Felicity. She looked appealingly at Martin, who smiled encouragingly at her and said, 'It has been pretty obvious for quite a while that you two are very fond of one another, I'm happy for you if that is what you want.'

'Hang on a moment,' said Mel, 'he's married, Mum.'

'Yes he is, technically,' said Felicity.

'Well, technically or not, how can you be sure he is not just messing about? His wife is in Australia, isn't she?' Felicity nodded. 'Well, maybe he is just marking time before he goes out there.'

'Stop it, Mel,' Martin said.

'Actually,' said Felicity, 'amazingly, we have his wife's blessing, she knows all about it and she ...' she hesitated, 'well, I haven't spoken to her myself, I don't know whether you would say she is happy about it, but she is certainly accepting that Keith will not be making his life in Australia but staying in Cornwall with me.'

'What do his children think?' Mel asked.

'We don't know yet,' said Felicity, 'we suspect his son will be fine, we don't know yet about his daughter but we're hopeful that if they both know that their mother accepts the situation, then there is no reason why they should not do so too.'

'Other than the fact that they will hardly ever see their father,' said Mel.

'We can visit,' said Felicity.

'That is going to be a bit awkward, isn't it?'

'Oh Mel, I don't know, I just don't know. Can't you even be a tiny bit supportive?'

'I think it is very fitting,' said Martin, 'moving from one upholder of the law to another.'

'What do you mean?' asked Mel, sharply.

'Your mother was married first to a lawyer and now she has taken up with a policeman.'

His attempts at levity fell on stony ground. 'I don't know what Dad would think, not much I imagine,' said Mel.

'Mel, your father has been dead for nearly eight years. Losing him was awful, I mourned him for years, I still do, he will always be in my thoughts. I had completely reconciled myself to being alone for the rest of my life, but then Keith came into it and

271

I ...' she hesitated.

'Spare us the details, please,' said Mel, her voice hard and angry.

Abruptly Felicity stood up. 'I'm sorry, Mel, but I am not going to stay and listen to this. I would have thought you could have been happy for me. I am still going to babysit your children if that is what you're worried about. Nothing has changed, it's just that I don't now have to spend the rest of my life alone. Thanks for supper.'

'Don't go,' said Martin, standing up too. 'Don't go like this.'

'I'm sorry,' said Felicity, feeling the threat of tears. 'I was just hoping for some support.'

Mel remained stubbornly silent and, whistling for Harvey, Felicity made for the front door. Martin followed.

'I am sorry,' he said, 'I'll walk you to your car.' He slipped an arm through Felicity's. 'It's just she was very fond of her father.'

'I was very fond of her father,' replied Felicity, angrily.

'I know, I know,' said Martin. 'For what it is worth, I am absolutely delighted for you. I think Keith is a splendid man and I am sure he will make you very happy, you'll make each other happy. I couldn't be more pleased.'

'Oh Martin,' said Felicity, stopping and

throwing arms around his neck, 'thank you, that is just what I needed to hear.'

Because she had left Mel and Martin so early in the evening, by the time Felicity had driven home and walked Harvey around the town, it was still not quite ten o'clock. She thought about Keith driving through the night, hoping he was not too tired, that he would not fall asleep at the wheel – he's a policeman, he's responsible, he will stop if he's tired, she told herself firmly. She felt restless and very upset by Mel's reaction and suddenly she knew what she had to do. She dialled Jamie's number and he answered almost immediately.

'I know what you're ringing about,' he said.

'Do you?' said Felicity.

'I've just had Mel on the phone bending my ear.'

'Oh, she is the limit,' said Felicity, 'I told her I hadn't spoken to you yet. I wanted to tell you myself.'

'Before you say any more, Mum, I do not share Mel's view and, I gather, neither does Martin.'

'You don't?' said Felicity, with a great sigh of relief.

'Not now I know that he is serious about it all, that he is leaving his wife, and that his wife is happy about it. So long as the relationship has a long-term future, then it's great.'

'Good lord, you're sounding like my father,' said Felicity, relief coursing through her.

'I would like to get to know him properly,' said Jamie, 'maybe we could come down and visit?'

'He is on his way to Boston at the moment,' said Felicity, 'but he is retiring soon. If you don't make it down here we will come up and see you then. Are you really alright about it, when you think about Dad and everything?'

'I'm fine,' said Jamie, 'you were going to be such a burden in your old age and now we have somebody else to take the strain. What a relief!'

'I love you, Jamie.'

'I love you too, Mum. He is a brave man, this Chief Inspector Penrose, taking on a mad woman like you, I hope he knows what he is doing.'

'To be honest,' said Felicity, 'I don't think he has a clue.'

'Probably just as well,' said Jamie. 'Will you marry, do you think?'

'We haven't got that far,' said Felicity, 'probably not, maybe, I just don't know.'

'Well, just make sure that if you do get married, you invite me to give you away, it will be a blessed relief.'

'You're a bad boy,' said Felicity, fondly.

Driving along the dark, almost deserted motorway,

274

Keith allowed his thoughts to drift away from the case and dwell instead on Felicity Paradise. Everything had happened so quickly and was so entangled with work that he had not had a chance to really absorb the momentous changes in his personal life. Barbara's gesture had been amazing, compassionate, considerate, but he knew it was not noble, he knew she did not really want him to be a full-time part of her life any more. She was rebuilding her life in a new country on her terms and he really was no part of it. The relief was huge and he realised suddenly that the fantasy that he had carried with him, for what seemed like years now, of having Felicity as an ongoing part of his life was within his grasp, was in fact already a reality. He felt a surge of something deep within him that at first he did not recognise and then realised it to be pure happiness.

26

The little girl sat high up on the beach watching the great waves come crashing in, they were the biggest waves she had ever seen in her life. With Mummy and Daddy each year they went on holiday to Salcombe. The waves there were little, tiny compared with these. They frightened her, the power, the noise, the spray which came drifting up the beach towards her. The sun was shining but she felt cold. She felt better, no longer sick, no longer so tired but she was cold, miserable and frightened. She looked up at Miss Reeny who was standing beside her gazing out to sea.

'I want to go back inside now,' she said.

Miss Reeny held out her hand to pull her up.

'Come on then, I'll take you home.'

The little girl ignored the outstretched hand and stood up, dusting the sand from her clothes. 'It's not home,' she said, 'home is with Mummy and Daddy in London. I don't like this place and I want my Mummy.' She turned on her heel and began struggling up the shifting sand on the beach. Miss Reeny caught up with her and placed a hand on her shoulder which the little girl attempted to shake off.

'I used to look after your mummy once, when she was small.'

Fiona frowned at her.

'Did you, why?'

'I just did, she was a lovely little girl, so kind and gentle, she and I were best friends.'

The child saw this information as the rebuke it was intended to be. 'I don't know why Mummy liked you, I don't like you, I hate you,' she said, and continued wrestling her way up the beach back towards the house.

Keith Penrose's day was confusing. He was exhausted to start with, having driven through the night, and it was disorientating to arrive in Boston at more or less the same time as he had left England, half a day having disappeared out of his life. He was met by a young policewoman called Judy who was taking him to a small police substation actually on Cape Cod, rather than going to central Boston. There he was to meet Major Bob Roberts who was in charge of the case. As if life wasn't weird enough, as they travelled down the main central highway onto Cape Cod, Keith saw signposts to very familiar places such as Truro, Falmouth, Helston. Bob Roberts was waiting for him and showed him into his office. He was a huge man, six foot four inches tall at least and broad with it. Keith could not imagine anyone so clearly overweight being in mainstream policing in the UK. Bob Roberts pumped Keith's hand. He had an iron grip which made Keith wonder whether he was fitter than he looked.

'It is good to meet you, Danny has filled me in. My name is Robert Roberts – I know, I know, I've heard all the gags, every gag everyone has ever thought of – like my parents couldn't be bothered to think of a name etc, etc. I look at it this way, I'm like New York.'

Keith frowned, trying to concentrate. What was this man talking about?

'So good they named it twice,' said Robert Roberts and gave a huge guffaw of laughter. 'Call me Bob.'

'Call me Keith,' said Keith.

'Now as I see it,' said Bob, who obviously wasted no time on anything, 'we've got to surprise this guy and be careful because there could be a little girl he's got kidnapped and she mustn't come to any harm? I don't know how you Brits do things, but here we are very keen on dawn raids when they are all muzzy with sleep and not thinking straight.

So my suggestion is I get Judy to take you to your hotel to get some sleep and we start the day at four a.m. tomorrow.'

'I don't want to leave it that long,' said Keith, 'Thomas Johnson is a powerful man, with friends in high places. Supposing he has picked up on the fact that you have been making enquiries about him? It is not impossible.'

'Unlikely,' said Bob.

'I agree,' said Keith, 'but not impossible. I'd rather move sooner rather than later. I could never forgive myself if he …' He let those words hang in the air.

'I get your drift, Chief Inspector. How about this then, how about we wait until after dark? If there is a kid involved she will probably go to bed early so everyone will be at home. We wait until the lights go out and then we go for it.'

'That would be better,' said Keith.

'So same scenario applies, alright? Judy takes you to your hotel. You look exhausted, you have some sleep and something to eat and we meet back here at, say, nine p.m. and then go and stake it out. I'm arranging for a social worker to be on hand.'

Keith frowned. 'A social worker?'

'A female for the little girl, assuming she is there. We need someone to take care of her. Now, I gather you have met this guy, tell me what you know about him.'

Keith thought for a moment. 'He is old and not very quick on his feet, but he is clever, very clever. I bet he will have a plan in case he is raided.'

'Right,' said Bob. 'Anything else?'

'He goes to bed quite early, at least he did when I saw him, and he likes his drink. He is not a drunkard, nothing like that, but he enjoys fine wines. Chances are if we catch him just after he has gone to bed he will have put away a few glasses of wine. Do we know who else is living in the house?'

'No, we were instructed by Danny to go softly, softly, so we haven't been anywhere near the house ourselves, just established that he owns it and that he is there at the moment, by making enquiries through the mailman, that kind of thing. Tell me, do you think he is armed?'

'I would think he certainly could be,' said Keith.

'OK, I'll make sure the boys all have their pieces.'

'I know we have to protect the little girl as best we can first but it would be good if it didn't end up too violent, not a shoot-out.'

'You see too many American cop shows, right?' said Bob, with one of his huge laughs.

'I don't know if they have told you the full story but during her kidnap her mother and baby brother were brutally knifed to death. We are fairly sure she, Fiona, wasn't in the room at the time but we don't know that and we certainly don't know what she heard. She is seven, she has got her whole life ahead of her, we need to try to send her forward into that life with as few bad images as possible.'

'You're a nice guy, Keith Penrose, I'm going to like working with you,' said Bob. Keith shrugged his shoulders awkwardly. 'Danny tells me you have been involved with this case a long time.'

Keith nodded. 'Forty years.'

'Jeez.'

'The first double murder which involved Fiona's mother being kidnapped happened during the first year of my career. We never found the little girl and we never found the murderer, it has haunted me ever since. I am just a few weeks off retirement now, I would give anything in the world to solve this one.'

'Well, Chief Inspector, I see it my solemn duty to send you into a happy retirement,' said Bob, giving Keith a playful tap across the shoulder which nearly sent him spinning to the floor.

It is amazing what a shower, seven hours of straight sleep and an enormous meal can do for a man. He still felt strangely wobbly and disorientated, but he was ready. The meal presented to him had been extraordinary. You could imagine a man like Bob Roberts tackling it but its sheer size astounded him, there appeared to be every sort of breakfast dish on his plate – eggs, bacon, sausages, waffles, tomatoes, mushrooms and fries, piled so high as to have fed a family of six. Keith was quite impressed with himself for managing nearly half, washed down with a pint of coffee, good coffee. Judy picked him up from the hotel at eight-fifteen and they drove to the police station and picked up Bob Roberts. Dusk was settling onto the freeway as they joined it, heading down to Cape Cod.

'So I understand from Danny that the nearer to Boston the smarter Cape Cod is.'

'More or less,' said Bob, 'there are some fairly interesting types right at the end and it kind of deteriorates as it goes down. Your guy is over half way down which, when you compare it with the kind of apartment he lives at in Washington, doesn't fit. You will see what I mean when we get there.'

'I am fascinated by these Cornish names,' said Keith, as they passed another signpost to Truro. 'It makes me feel quite at home.'

'How come?' Bob asked.

'I'm a Cornishman, I live and work in Cornwall. These names Truro, Falmouth, they are Cornish names.'

'Oh,' said Bob, 'so you have a Truro in England, right?'

Keith decided not to pursue the subject any further. 'How many men are you involving in this operation?' he asked.

'We've got eight cars with three men in each, they are all armed. We have a dog and a dog handler just in case we need it and we have paramedics on standby and the social worker will be in one of the patrol cars.'

'And you are confident that they won't be spotted?'

'Absolutely, we are the only vehicle going to be close to the house, I'm controlling everything from here. I'm sitting in the back of the car right now to be sociable, but once we get to the house I'll be sitting in the front in charge of the operation. We'll move when you and I agree it is right to do so, then the officers will abandon their cars and move forward on foot. No one in the neighbourhood is going to be suspicious, we have located the cars very carefully.'

'It sounds like a lot of planning has gone into this,' said Keith gratefully.

'More than normal,' Bob grinned at him. 'For two reasons – one, there is a child involved, second we aim to impress some high-flying Brit policeman that we know how to do things.'

Keith grinned. 'I'm impressed already, good man.'

The wait was tedious and nerve-wracking. Thomas Johnson's house was about as anonymous as it was possible for a house to be. It was a clapboard structure, right on the beach and while it wasn't dilapidated, it wasn't smart either. Bushes protected the garden behind it. It looked like tamarisk – what was this link with Cornwall, Keith thought, I'm going to have to find out. They parked up a little way from the house along the shoreline from where they could see the lights of the house reflecting on to the beach. The waiting seemed endless. Keith moved from excitement to despair. This whole operation was based on nothing more than a hunch, he was going to look an idiot so far as his boss, the Met and these American policemen were concerned and above all he would be letting down Ian McAllister and his daughter. There was no real evidence at all to link Thomas Johnson to Fiona's disappearance other than a chance remark of his daughter's flatmate and the coincidental use of a name. That was it, that was all – there was this huge fuss and expense for what? Just when Keith's paranoia was about to settle in permanently, the lights went out. Bob got his men out of their cars, there was no one to be seen, no movement but he had them edging forward until they were surrounding the house. Still Keith could see no one.

'What do we give it, half an hour for them to go to sleep?'

'I should think so,' said Keith.

The minutes ticked by.

'OK Keith, time's up! This is your show, you give the order.'

Keith took a deep breath. 'Let's go,' he said, in a surprisingly confident voice.

As Keith and Bob ran up the pathway to the front door – Bob was surprisingly agile on his feet – six police appeared in front of them, two with a battering ram. No one broke stride, they simply crashed the ram into the front door, it collapsed like paper, and the cops streamed in. Three made straight for the stairs, the other three to the back of the house. Bob followed them up the stairs. There was a darkened room to the left of the front door, a sitting room, some instinct took Keith that way. At the doorway Keith fumbled for a light switch, found one, and clicked it on. Thomas Johnson was sitting in an armchair by the remains of a dying fire. He looked smaller and older in the weeks since Keith had last seen him, a diminished figure.

'Ah,' he said after a moment, 'of course, if anybody was going to work it out, it was going to be you, Keith.'

Three policeman burst into the room. 'Is that

the guy?' one asked Keith. Keith nodded. They had Thomas out of the chair in seconds and handcuffed. They were rough and Keith didn't like it, but nothing mattered except the child.

'Where is she?' Keith shouted at him. The police went to bundle the man out of the room. 'Stop!' Keith shouted. 'Where is she, Thomas?'

Thomas nodded to a key on the table by the fireplace.

'Back room, downstairs, she is OK.'

Keith picked up the key with a trembling hand and ran down the hallway. He could hear the sounds of crying. There was a door at the end and he put the key in the lock and turned it. A little girl sat on her bed, sobbing, she was in her nightie and the bed was awash with cuddly toys. Keith turned on the light. The little girl screamed, rubbing her eyes against the brightness. He went straight to her and she flinched back against the pillows.

'Is your name Fiona?' Keith asked.

She nodded.

'I am a friend of your daddy's,' Keith said, 'my name is Keith, I've come all the way from London to rescue you. Would you like to go home now?'

The sobbing stopped, the child regarded him with big blue eyes, her fair hair tousled and tumbling down to her shoulders, she looked very small very fragile and very alone.

'You can take me home?' she asked, tremulously. Keith nodded, opened his arms and she threw herself into them.

The social worker was called Tilly, a lovely open-faced young woman with a friendly smile and an endearing dimple. Keith warmed to her immediately and could tell Fiona liked her too. Keith had stayed with Fiona until the social worker had arrived and now she still did not seem to want him to go, so he sat on the edge of the bed and after a little while, Bob came into the room.

'There was just an elderly woman upstairs and she was the only other person in the house, we've taken her away too.'

'Miss Reeny,' said Fiona, 'she is horrid, I hate her.'

'Well, you won't have to see her again, sweetheart,' said Bob, 'you're going home.' Turning to Keith, he said, 'I didn't tell you before, because it seemed like bad luck, but I've booked a double bedroom for Tilly and Fiona at the same hotel as yours, Keith. They can stay the night there and we will get them on the first plane we can in the morning.'

'You want me to stay then?' Keith asked, disappointed; he wanted to take this little girl home himself.

'Afraid so, my view is you are going to get more

out of Thomas Johnson than the rest of us.'

'Fair enough,' said Keith.

'Let's go then, sweetheart,' said Bob, 'you get to ride in a police car, you are going to stay the night in a hotel and then it is home you go.'

'If you gentlemen would leave us,' said Tilly, 'we will find some clothes for Fiona.'

'Just a moment,' said Keith; he glanced at his watch and felt in his pocket for his mobile. 'Let's see if we can talk to Daddy,' he said to Fiona. He scrolled down until he came to Ian McAllister's name. It was five o'clock in the morning but Keith imagined that the man was still not sleeping and he was right. On the third ring he heard Ian's voice.

'Ian,' said Keith, 'we've got her and she is safe.' He heard a sharp intake of breath.

'Keith, is that you? Where is she, where are you?'

'You are never going to believe this,' said Keith, 'but we are on Cape Cod, you know, the Cape Cod in America near Boston but she is perfectly alright and she is coming home to you tomorrow.'

'They haven't hurt her, she hasn't been ...' He couldn't say the words.

'She is perfect, she is OK, I'm sure of it.' Ian began to sob. 'Pull yourself together man, there is someone here you need to talk to.' He handed the phone to Fiona.

'Daddy?'

Tilly and the two policemen got off the bed and moved to the other side of the room.

'I love happy endings,' said Bob.

Keith looked up at him and smiled. 'Thanks, that was a great operation.'

'Nothing to it, was there?'

'It could have been awful.'

'It could have been, but it wasn't.'

The three adults were silent for a minute, just in time to hear Fiona say. 'Can I speak to Mummy now?' Keith winced, how was Ian going to handle that? There was a brief exchange and then ... 'Love you Daddy, tell Mummy and Ed I love them too. See you tomorrow. He wants to speak to you.' Fiona said, holding out the phone to Keith. In the last few minutes she had been transformed into a normal little girl, not the sobbing and frightened waif of just minutes ago.

'Thanks,' said Keith. 'Ian?'

'Can you put yourself some distance between you and Fiona?'

'Of course,' said Keith, 'we've been ordered out of the room anyway. She is going to get dressed so that we can go to the hotel.' He walked through to the sitting room where, until recently, Thomas Johnson had been sitting by the last of the fire.

'What's up?' Keith asked, knowing full well.

'You heard didn't you? She asked to speak to her mother, she clearly knows nothing about the murders, your friend Felicity was obviously right. I want you to make sure that no one else tells her but me. Will you make sure that the social worker says nothing nor any of the policemen? She must hear that her mother and her brother are dead from me and no one else.' The demands of parenthood, Keith thought, of course he would have felt exactly the same in the same circumstances. To have to tell your child the most awful news she would ever hear in her life: a nightmare, but of course Ian could trust no one else to do it but himself and he was right.

'Are you going to do it alone?' Keith asked.

'I don't know, I haven't thought it out yet. I can't believe she is safe, Keith, thanks, thanks so much. You will tell me all about it, though obviously not now.'

'Of course I will tell you all about it,' said Keith. 'I was thinking, there is a man at the Met, his name is Graham Sinclair. I am going to ring him as soon as I can to tell him what has happened. I am sure he can put you in touch with a child psychiatrist who could either be with you when you tell Fiona or at least give you some advice as to how to handle it. Fiona is not going to be back until tomorrow evening which is bad timing from a child's point of view. Maybe you should stay the night at the airport because it will be too late to go home. I don't know, it's a tough one.'

'That's a good idea, Keith. Actually we have a friend who is a psychiatrist and I am sure she will be able to put me in touch with someone specialising in children.'

'Fine, shall we ring you again tomorrow morning, our time that is, which will be about lunch time for you when we know the flight. I know the police will have it all sorted but Fiona would probably like to tell you herself.'

'I'd like you to do that please, Keith, because unless I hear her voice again, I'm going to imagine this is all a dream.'

When Keith came off the phone, Tilly and Fiona were being escorted to a police car, Fiona gave him a cheerful wave. Bob came over.

'Keith, can I have a word? I'm trying to get them out of here quickly before the press get wind of what is going on. Have you ever met the child?'

'No,' said Keith.

'So you can't formally identify her?'

'Not as such,' said Keith, 'but I have seen plenty of photographs of her and I can confirm she is a dead ringer for the little girl whose photographs hang all over the family home. Is it going to be a problem getting her out of the country? She really needs to be reunited with her father quickly under the circumstances.'

'No, I don't think so, I just thought we could fast track it if you had actually met her. I'm aiming to get her on the plane tomorrow morning. Don't worry, we'll fix it this end. So far as Thomas Johnson is concerned, we're obviously not going to question him tonight. He is an old man and we'll get nothing sensible out of him at this hour. My feeling is that I should shake him down a bit tomorrow morning and then, unless I get a full confession out of him, I'll have to wheel you in. Is that OK?'

'Yes,' said Keith, 'I'd like to see Fiona off at the airport unless you want me at the station earlier?'

'No, we've taken him to Boston in any event so if you go with Tilly and Fiona to the airport, a car can bring you on to the station afterwards.'

'That's perfect, thanks.'

By the time Keith arrived back to the hotel and crawled into bed it was after two in the morning. He glanced at his watch, did the calculation and dialled Felicity's number.

'Where are you, what's happened, are you alright?' she said, all at once.

'In Boston, we've got her and yes,' he replied.

'You've got her, is she alright, is she safe?'

'She is absolutely fine.'

'Oh my God,' said Felicity, 'oh well done, I'm so proud of you. Was it dangerous, difficult?'

'No,' said Keith, 'it went surprisingly well. We went in all guns blazing, but only metaphorically speaking. We had no problems at all. We rounded up Thomas Johnson and an old lady who was there as well, presumably to look after Fiona. Thomas told me where the key was to Fiona's bedroom, I unlocked the door and there she was.'

'And is she in a terrible state?'

'No,' said Keith, 'she calmed down pretty quickly once she realised we had come to rescue her and take her home. The big horror though is yet to come.'

'What's that?' Felicity asked.

'She doesn't know her mother and brother are dead yet. You were right, she wasn't in the room.'

'You're not telling her?'

'No, no, it's Ian's job, he wants to do it and he is going to take some advice. Hopefully she and her social worker will be on a plane home tomorrow morning, it's just a question of working out the best way of telling the poor child. Well, there isn't a good way, is there, it's a nightmare.'

'But you got her, Keith, she is safe.'

'Yes, I can't quite believe it.'

'Have you told the Met yet?'

'It's my next call,' said Keith, 'and in answer to your question, no, I am not going to gloat. They are probably going to be bloody angry with me for not patching them in on what I was doing, but sitting there in that car waiting for the time when we could launch our raid on the house, I really thought I had made a fool of myself. I really thought that this was a complete wild goose chase and we were going to end up breaking into Thomas Johnson's house and looking complete fools. After all, it was just a hunch, a lucky hunch, and to be honest if I hadn't been coming up for retirement I don't think there is any way on God's earth that my "Super" would have sanctioned it. I think he did it because he was feeling guilty.'

'He is going to love it now, isn't he?' Felicity said.

'Yes,' said Keith, 'yes, he certainly will.'

27

Keith sat in the back of the police car as he was driven from Boston Airport to the Boston police station where Thomas Johnson was being held. He had been deeply moved by his parting with Fiona McAllister. He imagined that at some time during their time together Tilly must have told Fiona that it was Keith that had engineered the rescue. They also had another conversation on Keith's mobile with her father before the flight was called. Either way, Fiona clearly saw Keith as a friend and someone to trust. She had thanked him formally, shaking his hand and then holding Tilly's hand, flanked by two police officers, had started towards the departure gate. Then she had stopped, turned and ran back to him, thrown her arms around him. He had held the little body against him for a moment, then he had crouched down to her level. 'I've been a policeman for a very long time, Fiona, and I'm getting old now and I'm going to stop work soon. In all my time as a policeman nothing has been more important to me than seeing you safe. Good luck, I will remember you always.'

She smiled at him, then turned and ran back towards Tilly. Keith never cried, it was years since he had felt moved to tears. He did not cry now, but there was a lump in his throat as he left the terminal because he had parted from a little girl full of hope for a future and hours from now she would have to know that her mother and little brother were dead – and there was no way around it and there was no way to help her.

He thought of his conversation with Felicity hours earlier; her support was a new experience for him, her interest in his work, her pride in his achievement and her longing for him to come home. He felt suddenly very humbled by his good fortune. His thoughts turned again to his conversation in the early hours of the morning with Graham Sinclair. Graham had been surprisingly complimentary; Keith had imagined a very difficult conversation but having explained that he had acted with his Superintendent's permission, all the heat seemed to go out of Graham and he simply congratulated him on finding Fiona. He was gratifyingly anxious to please, organising Fiona's flight back and promising to discuss any support requirements with Ian McAllister. He would do his best to see there was no press, they would take her straight out of the terminal, avoiding passport control through the VIP lounge and from there she would be whisked away. At the moment the press were not aware of what had happened but it would not be long before someone would alert them and then there would be mayhem. That was the last thing a traumatised little girl needed. The car drew to an abrupt halt. 'We're here,' said the driver. She jumped out of the car before Keith could react, and opened the door for him. 'I'll take you up to Major Roberts,' she said.

Bob Roberts jumped up from behind his desk, came around and shook Keith by the hand, Keith hoping desperately that his hand would recover full mobility one day.

'Well we've got him, Keith, but he ain't talking. The only person he is prepared to talk to is you. I kind of anticipated that would happen. He sees himself as some sort of star, some sort of hero. He is mad, a real nutter.'

'Strange,' said Keith, taking a chair. 'He didn't present like that, he seemed like a – well, grief-stricken family man when I met him forty years ago and when I came back a few weeks ago and interviewed him, he seemed like a really caring father and grandfather.'

'That means nothing,' said Bob, dismissively.

'You must have these cases in the UK. These guys go on television sobbing and wailing about their lost relative and all the time they are the ones that have put them in the grave. There is a certain type of person who can put on a great act. Sometimes I think they believe it themselves.'

'I know what you mean,' said Keith. 'To be honest Bob, I suppose I'm just angry that I didn't see it coming, that having spent quite a lot of time with him over a protracted period, I should have got the measure of Thomas Johnson.'

'Well,' said Bob, 'he's quite pleased you took your time. I wouldn't go so far as to say he is cocky but he is certainly very chipper for an old man in a difficult position. He wants to talk to you; he says he will talk to you and no one else. He hasn't denied anything, he hasn't agreed to anything, he simply won't talk until he talks to you.'

'Do you want to sit in on it?'

'No, no we'll leave you alone with him, we'll watch you of course and make sure you're safe.'

'I don't think he is a threat,' said Keith.

'I wouldn't be too sure,' said Bob, 'anyway we're taking no chances, right, there is something real creepy about him.'

'What about the woman,' said Keith, 'who is she?'

'Her name is Ann Reeny, she has worked for

Thomas Johnson since the dawn of time. She is clearly in love with him although it is obviously not reciprocated.'

'What is she, a housekeeper?'

'Yeh, guess so, she was looking after Fiona who she described as Mr Johnson's granddaughter. We're trying to get her to admit to having looked after the other little girl, but she won't at the moment. Do you want to talk to her before Johnson?'

'No,' said Keith, 'no, I'll leave her to you.'

The diminished creature that Thomas Johnson had appeared to be the night before had gone. While Keith wasn't expecting remorse, he had been expecting relief of some kind after living a lie for forty years. Instead, this morning, the man seemed positively jaunty, apparently revelling in being the centre of attention. He's mad, thought Keith, how the hell could I have missed that? He lowered himself into a chair opposite Thomas.

'So Keith, have you worked it all out?'

'Parts of it,' said Keith. There was no point in bluffing, the man was too bright.

'If you tell me what parts you've worked out we'll see how much progress you have made.'

'Mr Johnson,' said Keith, 'if I could remind you, you've been arrested for a very serious crime, a series of crimes, so I'll do the talking and you answer the questions.'

'I'm just so curious to know how far you've got, Keith, you can't blame me for that.'

Maybe it was best to play along with the man. 'OK,' said Keith, 'I believe you had your wife Caroline killed because she wouldn't bring the girls out to Washington. I expect she was afraid to do so because you hadn't officially adopted them and I suspect you hadn't officially adopted them because although charges were dropped, you were up on a rape case while you were still at school.'

'Very good,' said Thomas Johnson, 'absolutely spot on, so far.'

'So you admit to what, hiring a hitman, to kill your wife?'

Suddenly his face contorted, his anger something Keith had never seen before. 'She had no right to the girls, the girls weren't hers, they were *my* flesh and blood, my sister's children. She kept insisting she was their mother.'

'She had brought them up for seven years,' Keith said.

'*We* brought them up and she refused absolutely to come to Washington.'

'Why exactly?' said Keith.

'I had arranged passports; false documentation is easy if you've got the money, so we didn't even have to risk the adoption process to get them out of the country, but she wouldn't do it, she said she didn't want to go on living a lie, she said she wanted to legally adopt them but I couldn't risk that.'

'Because of the rape case?' Keith said.

Thomas nodded.

'I don't expect your wife knew about that,'

'No,' Thomas conceded. 'The girl was a tart, the case was dropped ...'

'I don't want to hear,' said Keith. 'What is the name of the hitman?'

'He is dead now, he was an Italian with Mafia links. He and his wife went to England but he botched the job.'

'I was coming to that,' said Keith. 'Why was Katie killed?'

'As I said, it was a botch,' said Thomas. 'Katie was in the room when Marco killed Caroline; Katie got in the way.'

'Where was Janey?'

'In the garden, apparently.'

'Marco, you say?'

'Yes, his name was Marco Bellini, I can't remember the name of his wife. He died a couple of years later in some sort of inter-gang power struggle.'

'You know,' said Keith, 'in the eyes of the law Marco Bellini may have killed two people, but his crime will be considered much less serious compared to yours. Yours is the true crime, planning and being prepared to pay for the execution of your wife. Don't you feel any remorse, particularly as your other daughter, niece, however you like to describe it, poor little Katie, died as well? I was there, remember, I saw what the guy did to them.'

'Katie's death was unfortunate,' Thomas conceded.

'Unfortunate!' Keith shouted, jumping to his feet and striding around the room. 'Unfortunate, hacking a seven-year-old to death?'

Thomas simply regarded him in silence and then said. 'When there was no sign of Janey, I thought you and Lewisham would put two and two together and recognise that she had to be with me, there was no other explanation. I don't know why you didn't work it out?'

'You had an alibi, you showed genuine remorse, we closed borders in case someone tried to take Janey out of the country.'

'By the time you and Lewisham arrived at the house, Marco, his wife and Janey were halfway to Heathrow and before you even thought of closing the borders, they were halfway across the Atlantic,' Thomas boasted.

'And you think that is something to be proud of?' Keith said. He was increasingly angry and was controlling himself with difficulty. 'So you brought Janey here and settled her into Cape Cod with Ann

Reeny to help look after her and you renamed her Moira after your mother. She went to school here?'

'Yes,' said Thomas, 'first to a small primary school on Cape Cod and then to Boston, she was a bright girl. Clever of you to make the link with my mother's name, that was a stupid mistake on my part.'

'And she accepted coming to live with you?'

'There were a lot of questions at first, but don't forget, I was her father, she knew me. It was different with this one.'

'What one, Fiona?'

'Yes,' said Thomas, 'she wasn't at all like her mother. She was very angry and wanted to go home all the time.'

'She had never met you, of course she was angry – and scared. What the hell was an old man like you doing taking on another seven-year-old?'

'You're right,' said Thomas, 'I wasn't up to it and neither was Miss Reeny. In that one respect it was quite a relief when you turned up; she was proving a real handful. Tell me, have you worked out what happened to the McAllisters?'

The coldness of the man, the cat and mouse game he was playing made Keith want to shake him until his teeth rattled, until he himself felt as scared as Fiona had done.

'Supposing you simply tell me what happened, Mr Johnson.'

'I'd like to hear your theory first.'

Keith didn't have a theory but he knew a woman who did. Maybe Felicity was right. 'You killed Moira because she was either blackmailing you or threatening to expose the fact that you had killed her mother and sister. I don't know why you sent her back to England, it had to be a risk.'

'She wanted to go,' said Thomas, 'she knew her mother and sister were dead. I'd made up a plausible enough story for her, she got a place at Durham University, she was a bright cookie so off she went. I explained away the change of name all along by telling her it was the best way to avoid publicity. I thought she would come back for holidays but she never did, I never saw her again. She was very ungrateful, I bought her a flat, put money in an account for her and all I got was an obligatory Christmas card. That was it. We spoke on the phone a couple of times but she didn't seem to want me in her life.'

'I wonder why?' said Keith, dryly.

'She didn't know then what had happened to her mother. That only came later.'

'How did it come about?' Keith asked.

'The internet, of course, the source of all evil. After Fiona was born she went back to work, but when the boy was born, with two small children she decided to work very part-time from home. She was messing about on her computer one day and found the story of her mother and sister's deaths and the hunt for her. She put two and two together and realised that I had to be behind it all.'

'Was she blackmailing you?'

'No, she didn't want anything; she just rang me one day out of the blue and told me she was going to report me to the police. I had to do something and I had to do something quickly.'

'So you had her killed?' Keith said, his voice flat with the horror of it. 'You raised this girl then you had her killed?'

'She was ungrateful, I see now she was like my sister, hard as nails, didn't give a damn about me.'

'You don't think that deep down she may have known all along you were behind her mother's murder? That's enough to put anyone off forming a close bond with you.'

'She had no idea until she spotted it on the internet, I am sure of that.'

'So you hired another hitman?' Keith said, wearily. The enormity of this man's crimes with his apparent lack of remorse was beyond anything Keith had ever experienced before.

'Yes,' said Thomas.

'Name?'

'Joe Boxer.'

'He presumably is still alive?'

'Yes.'

'Where is he based?'

'Washington.'

Keith glanced towards the viewing mirror. Someone would be on to that immediately in the hopes of catching the man before the story reached the press. 'We'll track him down and see if he can corroborate your story, though once again the law will consider the main crime to be yours.' He hesitated for a moment, then said, 'the little boy, Ed, was that another botched job?'

'No,' said Thomas, 'I paid for Moira and her son to be killed.'

'Why,' Keith said, 'why in God's name?'

'To make it look like a copycat, to confuse you.'

'You had your grandson – great-nephew – killed, to make the crime look more like the original one?'

Thomas nodded. 'When I realised that the little girl, Fiona, was the same age as her mother had been when she came to live with me, I thought maybe I could have another go at raising a child and maybe this one would be more grateful. I'm retired now and I thought it would be nice to have a young one running around, I had raised a child from seven before – me and Miss Reeny, I thought it would be nice to do it again and this time I wouldn't let her go to England, that was where I made my mistake.'

'But Fiona wasn't as pliable as her mother?'

'No,' said Thomas, 'she really seemed to hate me.'

'Small wonder,' said Keith. 'Did you tell her you were a relation?'

'We never got that far. Every time I tried to talk to her she shouted at me and asked for her mother. We didn't have one civilised conversation except at the beginning when she was still a little drugged.'

'You gave her drugs?'

'Only to get her here, she is fine.'

Keith stood up. 'Interview concluded at five past one,' he said switching off the tape.

'You don't want to hear any more?'

'Is there any more?' said Keith.

'What made you realise it was me? When you came over to interview me you didn't have a clue. I thought, when you arrived, that you had worked it out and then I realised that you had only come to sympathise at my loss.'

'Yes,' said Keith, 'what a fool I was. I suppose poor little Fiona was down at Cape Cod while I was being wined and dined by you.'

'That's right,' said Thomas, 'and she is not a poor little Fiona, she is another ungrateful child like her mother.'

'Grateful!' Keith spat out. 'Grateful! You killed their mothers and you expect them to be grateful to you!'

'They didn't know.'

'They probably saw something in you that I missed,' said Keith and he pressed the bell to be let out.

'When will we talk again?'

'Never,' said Keith, and he strode out of the room.

28

Keith caught the first available flight out of Boston which brought him into Gatwick in the late evening. He knew he would have to spend the following day being debriefed by the Met so he checked himself into an airport hotel. He was tired but also oddly dispirited. It had happened to him before – coming so close to evil was contaminating and he felt unclean in mind rather than body. He ordered room service and hunted around in the mini-bar for a small bottle of red wine. He had just received a rather unappetising club sandwich when his mobile rang. He looked at the screen. It was Barbara – had she changed her mind about everything, had something happened to one of the children?

'Dad, it's not Mum, it's me, Carly. I left my mobile on the beach, would you believe, so Mum has lent me hers for a few days. How are you?'

'A bit jet-lagged,' said Keith, 'I've just got in from Boston.'

'Oh yes, I heard about the case from Mum, did you solve it?'

'I think so,' said Keith, 'we got the little girl back, that's the main thing.'

'Well done, Dad! I'm sorry about your retirement being a bit premature, are you very fed up with it?'

'To be honest,' said Keith, 'I haven't had time to think about it but that's enough about me, tell me your news.'

'We're fine,' said Carly, 'I love being married, he is such a lovely man, Dad.'

'That's what I like to hear,' said Keith.

'Life's great. I'm sorry Will's not here to talk to you but he's all loved up.'

'So I hear, do you approve?'

'Absolutely, she is a stunner and really nice with it. Too good for Will, of course.'

'Of course,' said Keith, smiling at the sibling rivalry never far below the surface.

'Dad ...' Carly hesitated, 'I just wanted to say that Mum explained everything to me about how you guys are splitting up but staying friends and that you've got this new relationship.'

'Yes,' said Keith, cautiously.

'And I just wanted to say, Dad, it is fine with me and with Will, we are cool about it.'

'Are you sure?' Keith asked.

'Absolutely, Mum is fine with it, therefore why would we not be? You deserve some fun, Dad, you've worked so hard all your life – but you will come and see us, won't you, and bring Felicity, Mum says that's fine too.'

'Of course I will,' said Keith. 'Carly ...' he searched for the words, 'it means so much to me that you are happy with this.'

'Dad, shut up, I love you and that will never change.'

'I love you too,' said Keith, 'so very much.'

29

Twenty-four hours later, for the first time ever Keith did not get out of the train at Truro but travelled on to St Erth. Felicity was waiting for him. They hugged wordlessly and Keith climbed wearily into her car and she drove him straight into St Ives to Barnoon car park. It was a beautiful clear night as they weaved their way down through the streets to Jericho Cottage to be rapturously greeted by Harvey. Keith collapsed at the kitchen table and Felicity poured him a glass of wine.

'I imagine the last thing you want to do is talk about it?'

Keith nodded. 'I want to tell you all about it, I will tell you all about it but not tonight, if that's OK.'

'I expect the Met gave you quite a grilling?'

Keith smiled. 'They did, it was quite pleasing though.'

'I imagine it was, I hope you didn't crow too much.'

'No I didn't, I was the soul of tact. Not so my "Super" though, he was overjoyed that Devon and Cornwall had beat the Met at their own game. I've been told there is a damn good lunch in it which is surprising because it is not normally his style at all. I think everybody is a bit demob happy on my behalf.'

'How are you feeling about the whole retirement thing now you're going to have time to think about it?'

Keith shrugged. 'One day at a time. Hey, I had a call from Carly.' He told her all about the conversation and Felicity told him of Mel and Jamie's reactions. 'We have three out of the four approving,' said Keith, 'so I suppose that's not too bad. Do you want me to speak to Mel?'

'I think it might be an idea to speak to Mel *and* Martin, both of us together, I mean. Maybe we could invite them over for a drink or something?'

They gazed at each other for a moment. 'This is all starting to feel real, isn't it,' said Keith, 'we are actually going to be able to do this, be together, openly in front of the world, or more importantly in front of our families.'

'Are you getting cold feet, Chief Inspector?' Felicity asked.

'No,' he took her hand, 'and you?'

'No.'

'Do you want to get married?' Keith asked. 'There won't be any problem with Barbara, if that is what you want.'

'Goodness,' said Felicity.

'I could repeat the question on one knee, but I am so stiff after all the travelling that I might be stuck there all night.'

'I don't think we need to be married, do you?' Felicity said after a moment, 'and I think there might be a danger of rocking the boat. Our marriage means your divorce and divorce is a painful thing, however amicable the parting. We are so lucky to have so much family support, let's leave things as they are.'

'And that is exactly how I feel,' said Keith. 'You know something, Mrs Paradise, we are weirdly compatible.'

'You know, I was thinking,' said Felicity, 'when you retire I wonder whether there isn't some opportunity for you to continue to work, part-time anyway, on cold cases or investigations which, for whatever reason, there isn't the time or the resources to deal with – just on a sort of freelance basis, I mean.'

'You're not suggesting I become a private investigator like that awful little man who was following you?'

'No, no, of course not,' said Felicity, 'but you

did do better than the whole of the Met put together.'

'Yes, but bear in mind I had an inside track, I was there at the scene of the original murder.'

'But that wasn't the reason you solved it. You picked up on the fact that Moira had an American accent and that Thomas's mother was named Moira. That was totally unconnected with any pre-knowledge of the case.'

'I suppose so,' said Keith.

'Well, there you go then, a new career opportunity and maybe I could even help you sometimes.'

'Certainly, your theory about the second murder was the right one,' Keith said, 'and you were right too about Fiona. Thank God she didn't see her mother and brother murdered.'

'Where was she?' Felicity asked.

'The most mundane of reasons, she was in the loo. She heard shouting and screaming, came out of the loo door, was seized by the Joe Boxer character and bundled out of the house.'

'Do we know how she has taken the news of the murders?'

Keith sighed heavily. 'No, no we don't. She and Ian have been spirited away to his cousin's home on a fairly remote farm up on Dartmoor. I expect the press will find them in the end but at least it will give them a few days' peace.'

'I expect it will be a front page story tomorrow with you as a hero.'

'I hope not,' said Keith, 'I hope they keep me out of it. I've refused all interviews and left it to the Met press department to do what they will with it.'

'I bet the press will probably be pursuing you as well.'

'I doubt they will find me here.'

'Are you working tomorrow?' Felicity asked.

'No, they've given me a day off so I thought I might spend it hiding out here with you.'

'I think that could be arranged,' said Felicity, smiling.

'Now, for heaven's sake, can we please go to bed while I've still got the strength to climb down the stairs?'

'I think that can be arranged too, Chief Inspector.'

EPILOGUE

Saturday, 26 June 2010

It was a lot of fuss – much more than Keith had wanted, but as Felicity said his retirement party was as much for his friends and colleagues as for himself – and a party it certainly was, a big one, for so many people wanted to be there. It was held at the Budock Vean Hotel on the Helford, where guests could spill out onto the lawn and from the very beginning, it was obviously a police retirement party like no other. As George Staple said, it was a perfect reflection of the man.

The place was awash with children and a gloriously random selection of people, from the great and the good of the county to an old man of the road who had lived rough on the streets of Redruth. For many years Keith had kept an eye on him and made sure he was safe and now, after much persuading, he had moved into a retirement home and looked all the better for it.

Felicity's family were all there, of course, with Mel being surprisingly gracious. Josh Buchanan and her god-daughter Ellie, were down from Oxford. Now satisfied that Keith was not going to break Felicity's heart, Annie had given her blessing to their relationship and was 'chuffed to bits' to be invited to the Chief Inspector's retirement party.

George Gresham, no longer a boy, now a young man, was there with his grandparents, another lost child safe and secure. Violet Symonds and her son Andy came and what gave Keith particular pleasure was the arrival of Miles Irving, and on his arm, his fiancée Anya, both looking radiant with happiness.

Ian McAllister arrived with his daughter, Fiona, who instantly chummed up with Felicity's grand-daughter Minty. Ian still looked like a broken man but much more at peace. Fiona, with the wonderful resilience of youth, was full of chat and laughter.

Ian shook Keith's hand. 'You saved my life, Chief Inspector.'

Keith shook his head in denial.

'No really, I would have topped myself if you hadn't found her. Now I have a reason to live.'

Keith glanced across at Fiona who was running

around a chair chasing Minty. 'A very good reason,' he said, smiling.

As each guest arrived, Keith was astounded afresh at how many people wanted to wish him well but with all the fuss, he was aware that Felicity was oddly jumpy.

'What is it?' he asked, 'you seem very on edge.'

'I'm fine, I'm fine,' she said, 'it is a lovely party.'

'I know you had a hand in it and I am truly grateful.'

'I'm glad you're enjoying it.' She smiled at him, then suddenly looked across the room, her face instantly relaxed, the anxiety gone. He followed her gaze and there, standing in the doorway was his son, Will. 'I was so afraid he wouldn't make it in time,' Felicity murmured.

Will was searching the faces in the crowd and suddenly spied his father. He strode across the room and took his father in his arms in a great bear hug. 'It's just me here, Dad, but I am here for all of us, Mum, Carly, Graham, we love you and wish you all the happiness in the world.'

'Thank you,' Keith managed, 'thank you so much.'

Will turned to Felicity. 'We meet again under better circumstances than last time, I think. Am I allowed to hug you too?'

'You certainly are,' said Felicity, 'thank you so,

so much for coming.'

Keith looked at them. 'So you cooked this up between you?'

'Guilty as charged,' said Will. 'Felicity just felt that someone from your family should be here, and she is quite right, of course.'

'I can't believe it,' said Keith, 'how long have we got you for?'

'Just a couple of days, I'm afraid, I go back on Wednesday.'

'What a long way to come,' said Keith, 'for such a short time.'

'Worth every minute of it, Dad, looks like they are giving you quite a send off.'

The speeches were made, the toast drunk, the presentation given – a very generous collection of fine red wine that was supposed to form the basis of a cellar.

'That lot will never reach a cellar,' said Jack sagely to his wife Maggie.

Will made a short speech in which he highlighted the difficulty of being a policeman and a family man as well and how brilliantly his father had done in both the role of policeman and Dad. Then Horace Greenaway, the pathologist and Keith's boyhood friend, made a witty speech full of anecdotes. Yet when he came to propose Keith's health, his voice was thick with emotion. Even Superintendent George Staple seemed genuinely moved. It was all becoming too much for Keith, Felicity could see that, and when everybody went in search of food and to replenish their drinks, she took his hand and they walked down the path towards the river. Soon the sounds of the party died away and they were quite alone. They found a bench in the sun and sat down.

'It's all a bit overwhelming,' Keith said. 'It's not that I'm not enjoying it or appreciating it; too much emotion I guess.'

'You're a Celt, you are supposed to thrive an emotion,' said Felicity. 'If you were an old Anglo-Saxon like me I could understand it.' She squeezed his hand. 'I know Will's speech was a bit much for you.'

'Do you think he meant it?'

'Of course he meant it, he wouldn't have said it otherwise.'

'I wish I had found Janey,' Keith said, suddenly. 'I spent more time with Thomas Johnson than anyone, I should have seen it in him, I should have seen what he was capable of.'

'You were a young man,' said Felicity, 'and he was a very plausible liar and OK, you didn't save her but you saved her daughter. And if you are looking for a feel-good factor today, Keith, just look at Miles and Anya, that is something to be proud of.'

Keith nodded, unable to speak, and then gathered Felicity into his arms.

'And now what?' he asked.

'Now my love, we live happily ever after.'

NOTES

You may like to find out more about people mentioned in the text who feature in earlier Felicity Paradise novels. Read the novels below to find them:

Charlie Paradise's story is in *Letting Go*
Martin Tregonning's story is in *Letting Go* and each subsequent novel
George Gresham's story is in *Intensive Care*
The twins, Hugo Irving and Bob Barnes, feature in *The Silver Sea* and *In a Small Town*
Miles Irving's and Anya Cascescu's stories are in *The Silver Sea* and *In a Small Town*
Will Penrose's story is in *Smoke Damage*
Gilla's, Ellie's and Josh's stories are in *Beach Break*
Violet Symonds' and her son Andy's stories are in *In a Small Town*

ACKNOWLEDGEMENTS

It goes without saying, I need to thank my husband and children for putting up with my mood swings and burnt meals which are a natural fall-out of writing. I would also like to thank Rod 'the deckchair' for his professional help; Jeff in the Wharf Post Office for keeping me smiling and focused; Sally Gilbert, my faithful courier; Diana Palmer; Heather & Ivan Corbett and Kate Richards.

Above all, I would like to thank Jo Pearce – I really am so grateful to you for being prepared to keep our team going and deep apologies to your boys for taking up so much of your time.